For Old Times' Sake

For Old Times' Sake

Jahnvvi Kuumar

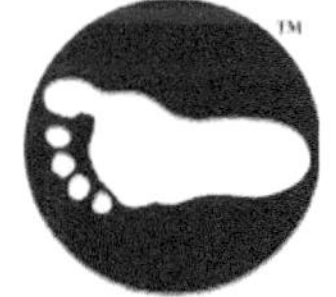

Bigfoot Publications
Because, there's a writer in everyone.

For Old Times' Sake
Author : Jahnvvi Kuumar

First Published by
Bigfoot06 Publications (OPC) Pvt. Ltd.
B-10,12 Shree Shyam Palace,
Sector 4,5 Chowk, Old Railway Road,
Gurugram, Haryana (122001)
Website: www.bigfootpublications.in
Email: info@bigfootpublications.in

First Edition : June, 2023
© Jahnvvi Kuumar

ISBN Print Book - **978-81-19201-52-5**

Although the author and publisher have made every effort to ensure the accuracy and completeness of information contained in this book, we assume no responsibility for errors, inaccuracies, omissions, or any inconsistencies herein. Any slights on people, places, or organizations are unintentional.

Printed in India

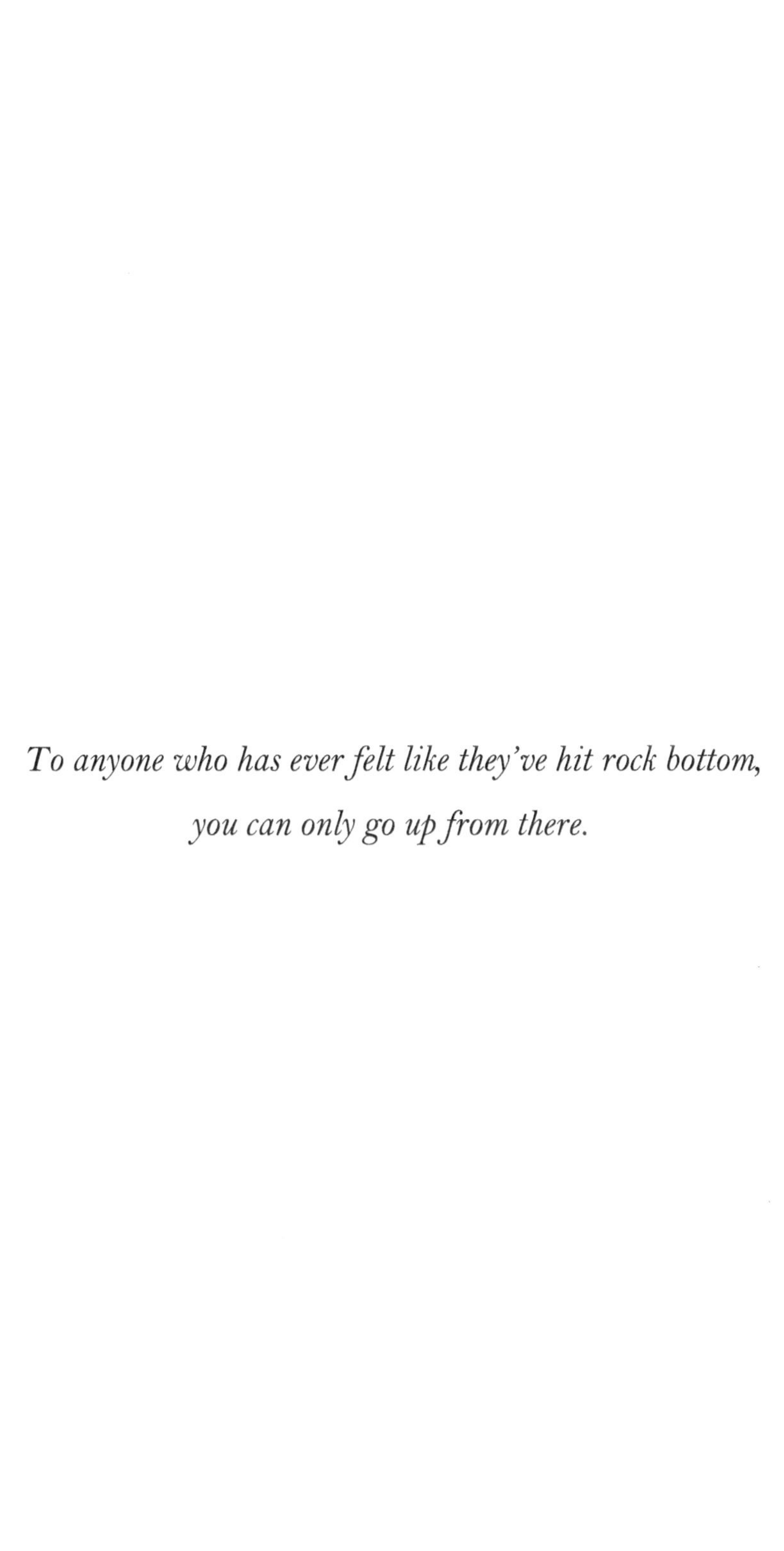

To anyone who has ever felt like they've hit rock bottom,

you can only go up from there.

Table Of Contents

PROLOGUE

Gave me no compasses, gave me no signs

It is a distinctly human act to attach meanings and connotations to the most arbitrary things and call it a sign. To chalk it up to the universe or the powers that be or simply your gut. I see the appeal, it can get pretty exciting seeing a physical manifestation affirm something (or someone) you were anticipating (or dreading). For a moment, feeling like something out there has got your back. Gatsby had his green light, the yellow umbrella in How I Met Your Mother, every movie made by Nora Ephron. It feels destined, fated, almost magical in a world so pragmatic, when you see a sign.

Well, let me tell you something, that is a load of bullshit.

My gut can't even digest dairy let alone give me cryptic, unsolicited hints about my future. The only angel numbers I see are the zeroes in my payslips and I'm not letting any higher powers take undue credit for that. Also, black cats have done nothing wrong to be on the receiving end of all the flak. Well, my black cat in particular is a terror of a roommate and takes after his namesake, Machiavelli, but I don't think he is the literal devil incarnate. The jury's still out on that one.

Anyway, signs and symbolism and good luck charms have lost all their meaning to me now. After months of endless research, grilling my poor real estate agent and visiting dodgy buildings to view even dodgier flats, I have finally signed the lease to my dream home. Or what I thought would be my dream home.

Flat 6 at 33 Ivy Hills has chevron-patterned hardwood floors, bookmatched marble countertops, a large bay window for Machiavelli and me to people-watch from; that would also let in all the sunlight London has to offer on the off chance it's not overcast and drenched. The neighbourhood is an oasis of serenity in an otherwise cacophonous capitalist cesspit and only a short tube ride to work when I do need to contribute to the cacophony of said capitalist cesspit to be able to afford living here. Everything looked perfect and my lucky number 6 kept popping up as if to reassure me that I did not need to think twice, this place was it. And now I want to teleport anywhere else from here.

"Woah, careful. Do you need a hand?" I hear someone say in front of me, beyond the three towering cardboard boxes I'm trying to balance in my arms as I manoeuvre my way from the lift to my front door. My eyebrows shoot up as goosebumps erupt all over me. This isn't just a 'someone'.

Squinting my eyes shut and cowering further behind my boxes, like a child with no object permanence playing hide and seek, I reply, "No! No no no, I'm good, I've got it all und-"

"Teddy?"

I could recognise that voice anywhere. It's the exact reason why I became a non-believer of signs in a split second and why I would much rather teleport to one of those dodgy apartments right now. Did all the signs and symbolism of the world take their collective PTO right before this moment? Right before I had to face him, after all these years.

Realistically, it only took a couple of seconds for me to start rotating to one side as he met me halfway and peeked sideways for us to finally see each other without any obstructions. But on a Saturday afternoon, in the hallway outside Flat 6 at 33 Ivy Hills, it felt like the clocks had stopped. The space-time continuum was most definitely at a standstill. How else was it possible that I was able to take in every single feature of his at my leisure and compare it to my last memory of him from six years ago. There was that number again, at least it snapped me back to reality this time.

"Wow, no one's called me that for years." I want to say to myself but decide to blurt it out instead. He is instantly frowning and tilting his head slightly to the right, like he always did when he was confused about something. It's as if I blurted out this thought too because he is instantly straightening himself and schooling his face to be the picture of utter nonchalance. "Oh, finally come to terms with Theodora huh? I always told you it was a beaut-"

"'No, just Thea now." I interrupt him rather harshly before we start getting too casual with one another.

"Right," he's studying my face as I look anywhere but directly at him.

Anyone looking at us right now could feel how palpable the tension was. We are standing right in front of each other but it would seem like we are playing a game of cat and mouse. If one of us is trying to catch, the other is trying their hardest to find an escape. We are chasing each other and trying to find a shortcut to the other, all while standing right here. I can't take it anymore, I have so many questions I want to ask him, so many things I want explanations to, but I go with, "So, do you live here?" Please say no, please say no, say you're visiting someone, please.

"Yeah, number 5, and you are in..?"

"6," I say, or at least try to say, with a tone and expression so neutral you could call me Switzerland. All the adrenaline, fight, hostility has seeped out of me in the last five minutes. We are neighbours. If nothing else, the universe is surely making up for the last six years in a bulk.

"Oh, right next door," he sighs and looks away "You sure you don't want any help?"

"No seriously, I'm almost done anyway."

"Okay, I'll see you around then?" I give him a nod and start walking towards my flat. This will be a lot to process. Unpacking be damned, I need a cold compress and a guided meditation video to deal with the after-effects of coming face-to-face with him out of the blue.

"Hey," he calls out and I turn around to face him again. And I hate that I did so with the reflex speed of a professional athlete.

"congrats on the new place and," he smiles languidly and pauses for a moment, his eyes slowly registering my entire frame "It was good to see you Te-Thea."

"Thank you Seb." I smile politely and rush inside my flat, slamming the door shut.

Machiavelli jumps from the couch and hisses loudly at me. "What? You would also slam the door on the feline-equivalent of Sebastian Henry." I unleash all my bottled-up emotions as I rapidly pace the room.

"The sheer audacity to pretend like we hit the reset button and became casual acquaintances all of a sudden, as if those two years we spent being the best of friends and six years being strangers happened in an alternate dimension. Tell me you wouldn't be seething with rage, seeing him act like after all this time we could go back to square one?"

Machiavelli purrs quietly and curls next to my feet in what I assume is an act of sympathy. Not the devil incarnate after all.

1

Like passing notes in secrecy

8 years ago

Am I in the wrong place? It did say 'Welcome Freshers!' on a rather huge banner outside this building. Plus, a group of 18-19-year-olds who I have definitely seen at another orientation event earlier this week are here too. I mean, of course they are, I inconspicuously followed them here. But it still does not feel right. If this is the university's icebreaker for freshers, then why does everyone look so much more…mature than me? Not necessarily older, but like they have their shit together. Everyone looks so self-assured. And worse, they are all already talking to each other. That petite girl next to the refreshment table is already cracking jokes, given how her company just started howling with laughter.

At least I can breathe a sigh of relief that I don't look too out of place. Most of the girls are dressed like me, in their jumpers and jeans. I spot a few dresses paired with sheer and semi-sheer tights but transitional weather be damned, I'm in full winter mode now. In fact, even my jeans couldn't brave the wind today. I was positively chilled to the bones and my tibia and fibula would still be freezing if it wasn't for the radiators behind me thawing them out of their misery right this second. I make a mental note to buy some of those fleece-lined tights they keep showing ads for online.

Sufficiently warm, I finally leave my very invigorating inner monologue and the corner near the entrance to inch closer to the refreshment table. I could go up to those people I followed here, on the opposite side of the room, but they already look like a pretty complete friendship group. The last thing I need is to draw their collective attention to introduce myself and then not even fit in and awkwardly stand in their periphery for the rest of the night. No, thank you. I would rather fill myself up with these free finger sandwiches, now that every penny counts.

The empty spaces in the room are slowly disappearing and the decibels are a little higher as more and more people strike up conversations around me. Whoever is in charge of the soft instrumental music in the background also wants their presence felt, increasing its volume just enough so there is no uncomfortable silence should two people not have anything to say to one another. I scan the room for any other solitary soul I can at least try to mingle with but it's a large space, and the exponential rate at which it's filling up with more established friend groups is no help.

I decide to stay put as the music fades out and an older gentleman walks up to the front of the room with a microphone, surely to give another iteration of the same welcome address I have heard over the last week. The people entering the room hurriedly try to find their bearings so as to not miss the speech and I have the urge to produce my own microphone out of thin air and tell them to relax. Use this energy when you're running late to the movies and don't want to miss the previews, or for flights when they have already announced the last boarding call or for that date you have been looking forward to, that wouldn't let you sleep a wink the night before. Not that I have any experience of the latter, but in theory it does sound like something you would want to cherish every second of. Mr receding hairline, whose shirt buttons are straining against his taut paunch to see another day, drawling on about this esteemed institution and our hard work and dedication is rather missable in comparison.

"Excuse me, sorry, sorry, passing through," someone whispers in the back, causing a commotion trying to make their way forward. I don't need to look back to tell they were successful in parting the packed room like the Red Sea as their voice gets closer and closer, only to end up beside me. His wet woollen coat brushes against my side as the air around me is suddenly tinted with a freshness of citrus and the unmistakable hint of London's smog-riddled rains. As I am trying to discern this new presence strictly through my nose when I could very well turn my face and look at him instead, I am rudely interrupted by the owner of these scents.

"So, what did I miss?" He asks me as if we know each other. As if coming to stand next to me was a deliberate move, even though I have never met this boy in my life.

"Uh… nothing much, the usual platitudes about new beginnings, etcetera," I say trying to act as casual as I can, like I wasn't just sniffing the air to make out what this stranger smelled of.

"Has he talked about the buildings yet?"

What? Do I need to come up with an escape route or at least try to distance myself from him? I may not be the most competent socialiser but at least I don't make small talk about buildings.

"Buildings…?" I reply as I feel people's eyes on us like it's the highest act of treason, daring to converse right now. So much for wearing my plainest jumper and jeans and not wanting to stick out in the crowd.

"Yeah, the different buildings on our campus," he keeps talking while looking straight ahead. I confirm that no buildings have been mentioned yet and finally turn my head to look at this strange stranger. My eyes are met with a decent face structure. Okay, I lie, a more than decent face structure. But a sharp jawline has absolutely no correlation to someone not being a psychopath. If anything, most true crime documentaries have taught me that it's always the charming and good-looking ones that turn out to be serial killers.

"Here it comes," he whispers under his breath and I am immediately on high alert. What is he on about? I am scoping out our surroundings but everything looks just as it was. In my hypervigilant state, I miss out on the speech for some time only to catch the tail-end of the sentence.

"…and the human sciences department is based on the South side in Perv Hall…"

Oh.

"…where you will get to study the wonders of the human body…"

Oh God.

Muffled giggles fill my right ear as the stranger manages to mumble, "Wait for it, it gets better."

"…led by Dr. Faartz."

I don't know how everyone else seems to be so composed because I am trying very hard to not burst into a cackle while a certain someone next to me has given up and is close to tears.

"He uses the same speech every orientation week," the strange boy says, finally turning to face me completely. "I missed it last year, there was no way I would miss it this time too".

"Oh, you're not a first-year?"

"Nope, second year of the supposed best years of our lives, though I don't see what the fuss is about. There's the freedom I guess but what about all the existential dread that comes along with it?" He rambles on as I get a moment to look at him properly. His dark hair is actually a shade lighter now that it's not wet from the rain anymore. The curls at the front are in a constant battle to curtain his forehead every time he moves his head while talking, which he does a lot. It's like the words are in a rush to escape his mouth. A mouth that he has bitten red, matching the colour his cheeks have turned from the arctic weather outside. He's cute. And he's still talking, so I decide it's time to interrupt him.

"You should probably introduce yourself," I catch his attention, "if you're planning to trauma dump and scare me before I even start university," I said and pursed my lips into a smile, the kind you do to seem polite when passing by an acquaintance in a foyer. The kind that says I'm a nice person and I think you are too but I would literally do anything else than stop and chat with you right now.

He chuckles, "Right, sorry, I'm Sebastian. Sebastian Henry. Second-year art history student. A sucker for funny innuendos and grappling with my purpose in life, but you already knew that. Now if you could introduce yourself so we could be partners in trauma dumping?" he says while squinting his eyes.

"Theodora Rossi. First-year communication and marketing." I tell him as we shake hands.

"Theodora. That's a beautiful name."

I scoff, "Thanks, I hate it."

"What, why? It sounds so regal, plus I've never met a Theodora before, but I bet you know at least three Sebastians."

I actually don't know any other Sebastians but he doesn't need to know that. Why should I stroke his ego over his perfectly regular name?

"It's not about that, it's actually the opposite. What's the point of having a unique name when your mother names you after herself?"

"Like that show, Gilmore Girls?"

"Exactly like Gilmore Girls!" He jumps a little as I cry out, not expecting him to bring up the reference I use every time I have had to tell someone my name.

"Was it for the same reason as Lorelai, it's sexist that only men name their children after themselves and all that? Because that's cool," he says with an intonation that makes me believe he actually does find it cool and is not just saying it for the sake of it.

"Well yes, and I was born before the show aired so my mom takes full credit for that. But I don't know if I fully believe her progressive intentions," I mock-whisper conspiratorially, "she is quite narcissistic you see." He hums as he crosses his arms and supports his chin with his right hand, as though we were discussing some very serious matters and the gravity of the situation was taking a physical toll on his face's ability to stay upright. His big, brown eyes were boring into me, waiting for whatever I say next, the next piece of the puzzle of me.

"Plus, at least Lorelai nicknamed her daughter Rory, I have always been Theodora. Just Theodora. So that's unfair."

"I could give you a nickname," he perks up. "We could come up with one right now."

This has to be the most unusual first interaction I have possibly ever had. A few minutes ago, I was ready to run away because surely he was a serial killer. And now suddenly, with him, there is an ease I have rarely felt before today.

"It is the most obvious one," he continues, breaking my chain of thought. "But what about Dora?"

"Like the explorer? What if I decided to cut my hair short and get bangs, the joke writes itself."

"Hmm, yeah that's a situational hazard waiting to happen, even if you carry a backpack or decide to adopt a pet monkey."

"I have been thinking of getting a pet, and monkeys are not out of contention yet so…"

"Dora won't work, plus you don't even look like a Dora to me." I wonder what he means by that. What do I look like to him? He has eyes that I would imagine have been described as kind by anyone who has met him. His eyes, that look like they know me better than they should, have not left mine since we started talking.

His eyes widen, "I've got it," he takes a pregnant pause as I look at him expectantly to deliver a masterpiece of a nickname.

"Teddy."

"That is what you come up with after we reject Dora?" Great, I look like a teddy bear to him, I got my answer.

"Wait, wait, wait, let me explain. I'm not calling you a stuffed bear if that is what you were thinking," Okay, mind reader, "it's just that if all the Theodore's of the world, mind you who are most probably fully grown, adult men, can be called Teddy, why can't you? For once Teddy would actually sound cute and match the person it belongs to," he says matter-of-factly. "So it's settled then, you're Teddy." I find it hard to battle a logic that includes being alluded to as cute, sue me.

"Let's see if it catches on, but I think I deserve to coin a nickname for you now."

"Sure, go ahead."

"Very unoriginal, but I would say Seb suits you just fine." It has that same air of coolness and benevolence that he exudes. Someone who would run through the rain to not miss out the university's dean saying perv and farts, but also someone who would befriend a stranger and put in genuine effort into giving them a nickname.

He nods with a smile, "I'll take it, Teddy. Seb and Ted has a nice ring to it."

I agree, "It does, as opposed to Theodora Rossi and Sebastian Henry."

"Oh yeah," he snickers, "the acronym of which would be…" he drags out his sentence hinting at me to decipher the joke he has already figured out.

It takes me a second as it dawns on me, "T.R.A.S.H." Our deadpan looks switch to a mix of disbelief and pure joy as we break into a fit of laughter. I get the chance to look around the room for the first time in a while as I notice the speech is long over and the room and its inhabitants have resumed to their positions from before. The same groups have congregated once again and the instrumental music is back on, the only difference is that I don't feel alone anymore. I am not alone anymore.

"What does that prophecise about the future of our friendship?" I ask him as we both come down from the laughter.

"Nah, nothing. You know what they say, one man's trash and all that," he says as we start walking towards the exit with an unspoken understanding that nothing else in this room could pique our interest. The irony is not lost on me that not only was I willingly leaving with Seb, instead of escaping from him how I thought I would have to, but he had inadvertently given me the same nickname as the serial killer Ted Bundy. Oh, how the tables turn.

2

You gave me everything and nothing

Present day

Light pours in from the bay window, prickling my eyelids as I groggily wake up on my couch, where I had dozed off last night after multiple failed attempts at figuring out the Ikea instructions to build my dresser. While blaming the instructions is completely rational, because truly, how many screws and bits and bobs does this dresser actually need? I would be lying if I said I wasn't a little distracted, preoccupied with replaying the event of bumping into a certain someone yesterday.

And if that wasn't enough, we share a wall. I can practically hear him moving around his living room. I think if I pressed my ear against said wall, I could even make out his breathing pattern, that's how thin this wall is. I'm only half-awake but I can tell he is shuffling around his kitchen, opening and closing his cabinets. As much as I don't want to care about my new neighbour, my mind betrays me and marches ahead.

I wonder if he still takes his coffee like before, does he still pour heapings of milk into it, that barely qualifies it as coffee and safely pushes it into flavoured milk territory? What would he be wearing right now? He always preferred comfort but knew what looked good on him, and that kind of self-assuredness just worked, he didn't need to follow any trends or subscribe to any aesthetic. He did buy every sweater vest that came into view though and swore he would not part with them until he died. Would he have upheld that declaration still? What are his plans for today? What does a grown-up Seb do on Sundays? Wait, what does he do for a living?

That thought hits me like a truck and pulls me out of my own thoughts. The Seb I met yesterday is not the Seb I knew. I have no idea who he is anymore and we are as good as strangers. I remember reading somewhere that it takes approximately seven years for all cells in the human body to regenerate and get replaced. I don't know how scientifically accurate that factoid is but it could be that even on a cellular level, Seb and I are completely different people than who we were eight years ago, when we first met.

It's weird how when you get close to someone, when you consider them your best friend, you do everything in your capacity to get to know them better.

Consciously or subconsciously, you pick up on things they like or dislike, you file the anecdotes and memories they share with you in your own heart, making it a piece of you as much as it is theirs. You start seeing trinkets in shops or posts online and your first instinct is how much they would like it. You read their horoscope before yours and if you're into it, you know their moon and rising along with their sun sign too. But you can detect a change in their mood without reading any predictions from the stars though, and most of all, you care. Maybe it's selfish or maybe it's selfless, who's to say? And what happens when this connection gets severed by some twist of fate? What are you to do with all this insight into one person when it doesn't matter anymore? When it is suspended in a moment in time like butterflies preserved in a display case. You can look at and admire them for what they are, but with the innate knowledge that their life, growth and purpose has been stunted. What better are we than Pavlov's dog, when we condition ourselves to get so attuned to another person so unconditionally.

Machiavelli meows at me, probably sensing that I said the word 'dog' in my head. Or he is just hungry. I pour his food into his bowl just as there is a knock at the front door. It's only my second day in this place so it could be literally anyone from this building and I would be none the wiser. I could pretend like no one's home and just not bother answering the door. Who even goes up to their neighbours anymore? Isn't that like an unspoken agreement in London, where we just pretend other people don't exist and just keep on carrying on? I give myself a once-over in the hallway mirror that I have yet to hang and decide to grant this person my presence today.

Matting my fly-aways down in a few short seconds, I peek through the peephole. Seb. Of course, it's Seb. I knew I had my finger on the pulse of London's sentiments towards social interaction. Seb was the anomaly. He is always the exception. But I can't even pull the disappearing act on him (akin to what he did to me six years back), since he's probably been listening to me through the thin walls too. His smile widens as I pull the door wide open.

"Good morning!" He chirps as I come face to face with him. I don't think he got the hint when I slammed the door on him yesterday, so I don't know what's the protocol here.

"Hi."

Is he here to answer the questions I haven't even asked him yet? Does he want to borrow a cup of sugar, he should know I would give him a cup of salt if he does ask that. Hell, does he want to be invited in, should I invite him in? What are the rules for interacting with your ex-best friend turned new neighbour, someone should conduct a MasterClass on that, I would happily pay them whatever asinine amount they ask for.

"I just," he struggles to find his words, and that's when I notice the potted plant in his hands. "I didn't welcome you properly yesterday, or congratulate you for that matter-"

"You did."

"Huh?"

"You did congratulate me, it was the last thing you said," I remind him. Guess he really didn't register the slamming door if he doesn't even remember what he said. Funny how it didn't occur to me how he must have felt seeing me. If I saw a ghost, he did too. If anything he looks like he is still in a daze given how he's taking his time choosing his words, taking me in and rubbing the terracotta pot with his thumb as a nervous tick, leaving the tiniest particles of its dust and shavings on the carpeted floor that I'm fixating on.

"Well, doesn't hurt to say it again," he punctuates it with another smile. He smiles too much, always did. The only difference is I don't find it that endearing anymore. "and I wanted to give this to you," He hands me the plant and adds with a cough, "Peace Lilies, they're ideal to keep as house plants apparently, easy to care for, don't need much."

"Uh… thanks." I say as I rotate and inspect the plant in my hands. Does he think I can't take care of a more difficult plant, what does this mean?

We stand there awkwardly for another few seconds because truly, what does one say in such circumstances, on a Sunday morning? I'm dying to ask him where he has been, why he decided to leave without telling me six years ago. But it feels wrong to dive into an interrogation as I'm holding a gift from him. But I can't do small talk, not with him. The harder questions will rot me on the inside if I'm asking him about work and the weather, but dodging and avoiding any real conversation. I want to shake him and scream at him but he is showing no signs of wanting to revisit the past. I want to shake him and scream at him because he is showing no signs of wanting to revisit the past. But I won't, because it's a Sunday morning and we are pretending to be cordial neighbours.

"Right, I'll leave you to it then. See you around," he says with half a wave as he quickly side-steps to open his own door and leaves.

He keeps saying that, see you around, does he actually want to because I really can't gauge how much more awkward we would get, especially without a potted plant acting as a buffer. Speaking of which, I place the Peace Lilies on my centre table and sit back down on my couch. Machiavelli is done eating and hops onto the table to scope out this new addition to his surroundings. When he attempts to lick the flowers I pull him to me as we both sit and stare at it in silence, not sure what to make of it. I pick up my phone to google the plant. As I'm typing my query, autocomplete suggestions pop up. One of them catches my eye, the symbolism of peace lilies. Clicking on it, I'm instantly made aware of the fact that Peace Lilies are common flowers for funerals. Fantastic. What is he trying to imply? I hope you DIE, my condolences in advance. Or is it symbolic of us? Rest in peace, Seb and Teddy. Here lies our friendship that cannot be resuscitated, please never bring it up again, don't even think of talking to me again. B-bye!

I click on another article, because I'm a masochist like that, and it offers a much simpler explanation. Like the name suggests, it says, Peace Lilies can be gifted as a peace offering. Hm. Sounds like a reach, but okay, whatever. As if Seb researched flowers and their meanings before choosing to give this to me. He probably just picked the first one he saw at the shop…who am I kidding, Seb puts in thought behind every single thing he does. Or did. Ugh.

I deleted my previous search and asked google what plant one should give to ask for forgiveness. The answer is white tulips. They symbolise renewal and repairing a relationship. There, that is what he should have got instead. We aren't at war for him to give the plant equivalent of a white flag, he may as well have extended a literal olive branch then. I am infuriated with him obviously, especially given his composed demeanour the two times I have seen him, but he should be the one giving me an explanation rather than me trying to look for his answers on the internet. He should be saying sorry for promising to meet me the day after he graduated, only to stand me up. For disappearing without a trace, without any explanation. For leaving me alone and stranded, in a world and time, I didn't know how to navigate without him. For making me question every single thing I had said and done, wondering how it was my fault. Blaming myself for not being a good enough friend, blaming myself for how I could give someone else so much power over my well-being. It's been a long time since and details get blurry as the passage of time progresses, but I will never forget that feeling of being lost. Of losing all sense of belonging.

Machiavelli escapes my hold and wanders near the flowers again. I don't stop him and wait to see what he does. And after a cursory glance, he just walks away. Tail swaying and eyes set on an abandoned cardboard box that previously held my packed belongings, he flops inside and curls into himself to take a nap. There is a lesson to be learnt there. So I get up and stop dwelling on trivial things that take up unnecessary brain space. I need to sort out this place today before the work week starts tomorrow. I should call and check up on Millie and also come to terms with the fact that I will have to see his stupid face from time to time and hear whatever he is up to whenever we are in our respective living rooms, and that's not a big deal.

Until I remember he was wearing a sweater vest this morning.

3

I just wanna know you better

8 years ago

"**L**et me get this straight, your sister's name is Millie."

"Yup."

"Which is not short for Mildred or anything…?"

"Nope."

"I'm having a very hard time figuring out which one of you is your mother's favourite child; the one who got the same name as her or the one with one of the most common names around."

"Hah," I roll my eyes because I know he knows that what he's implying is not true, "but my mom didn't name Millie, it was my dad. Though I'm like, 90 percent sure he took over because he was scared my mom would end up naming her Theodora, the third."

I had come to the library to start working on an assignment that I had been procrastinating on but Seb asked to tag along, and I doubt I'm going to get any work done now. Even though we are still talking about names, it's hard to believe it's already been over two months since the first day I met Seb. I have made some friends in my course but I think labelling them as 'friends' would be an exaggeration, given that we only talk in class and go our separate ways as soon as it's time to leave. So almost everyday, if Seb and I are not in our respective classes, we are hanging out with each other. It sounds like the biggest cliche but with Seb, it feels easy. It's only been a short time since we have gotten to know each other, but there is an ease, a sense of comfort around him. I can't pinpoint exactly what it is, maybe it's the fact that he just took me under his wing from the first moment, without the need for any uncomfortable introductions; your classic 'extrovert adopts the introvert' scenario.

He already knows things about me that I would dare not tell my friends from home. But I guess that's a normal experience everyone goes through. There is a unique sense of freedom in telling someone new your secrets, who you know has no connections or context to judge your past. Someone who cares enough to listen but not enough to pry and dig in for details. Of course, with Seb, it also comes with the territory of being a boy.

Not to generalise and stereotype here, but I doubt the things I tell him are taking priority over whatever topics preoccupy a 20-year-old boy's brain. Though one of which, I assume, is walking by us. Slowing down to take check out Seb, from head to toe and back up again, then disappearing behind a row of shelves.

"Um… hello," I nudged Seb's elbow in front of me, "Did you see that girl?"

He looks up in confusion, from his borrowed copy of 'What Great Paintings Say', his reading glasses slipping down his nose in the process, "Who?"

"The pretty girl who just walked by our table, she was looking at you. Basically eye-fuc-"

"Please don't say that."

"-but she DID!"

"Shhhh, we are in the library!"

I whisper, "But she did! She totally checked you out."

"Okay, thank you for that information but I don't know what to do with that," he shrugs.

"Well if she comes back, which I'm sure she will, talk to her."

"Teddy," he tilts his head to the side, "I'm not going to talk to someone just because they checked me out. That means nothing."

"Are you crazy? That means everything! You're literally reading a book about looking at paintings. That's what you do in museums right? You. Check. Paintings. Out." I enunciate each word for him, hoping it penetrates through his dumb logic.

"Well, sadly for us, painting can't talk. Girls can. If she wants to, she can come to say hi."

He goes back to reading his book stoically, adjusting his glasses to be level with his eyes again.

I take a beat and retaliate, "What if the poor girl couldn't speak, what if she's mute? You are being very discriminatory right now Seb," I sit back and pretend to be fascinated by my nail beds, "it's not a cute look on you."

Without looking up he replies, "She can use sign language, I know BSL."

"You know BSL?" I gawk at him. "How?"

"A kid in my school was deaf, a bunch of us learned it together so we could talk to him."

"That's so sweet. My classmates drew on a kid's face once, during a school sleepover, with a permanent marker."

"Oof, the duality of adolescence."

I hum in agreement as I notice in my peripheral vision that he is looking at me. I continue aimlessly moving my cursor on my laptop screen as he's still looking at me. Why's he still looking at me?

"For someone who claims to be an introvert and froze and ran away the first time a boy tried to talk to her, you're really adamant on me talking to some girl."

"Jeez, I was just trying to help," I look at his smirking face, "and I told you that in confidence!"

"It's still confidential, I'm only saying it back to you!"

"Nope, you can't use it against me, that's unethical."

He throws his hands up in surrender and slumps back into his chair.

"Can you teach me BSL though? I'd really like that"

"Sure Teddy," he nods, "that way you can communicate with your hands the next time you freeze up in front of a boy-"

"SEB!"

4

Your finger on my hairpin triggers

Present Day

Call me crazy but I actually like my daily commute in London. Some, or rather many, find it unbearable to travel during rush hours on the tube, squeezing and sandwiching between strangers, breathing in stale air and inhaling all kinds of odours. Brushing against all the different textures of people's choice of outerwear or bags, touching surfaces that have touched God knows how many strangers and substances. Entering the overpacked train's doors at your station feels like being devoured by a gluttonous monster, only to be spat out in record speed at your destination because, as it turns out, the monster couldn't keep it down. What I'm trying to say is, yes, it's gross. But if you happen to find a seat, or a corner to latch onto, and you're lucky or privileged enough to be commuting only for a few stops, it can actually feel nice. Some tube lines make the most horrendous noises and screech like actual monsters, but tune it out and there's a lull to it, a rhythm.

People like to take the bus or cycle on the busy streets because they get to look around and take in nature or the shops or people going about their days, and the tube obviously gives a traveller none of those offerings. But what it does give you, is a sense of detachment. All you see are the dark tunnels with the occasional yellow light sconces as the train takes harsh twists and turns. With no sense of the time of day, the happenings above ground or direction, it is akin to a liminal space. It can be a very introspective space. You can still people-watch, wonder what your fellow commuters are wondering about. You can read, listen to music or think about things endlessly. Or you can simply give in. Take a moment of respite and just be. Don't worry about anything, don't distract yourself to make the time pass with something. It can just be a moment to escape and exist, without expectations and impositions.

Before I can romanticise my tube ride any further, I have arrived at my stop. With my move, the journey to work has shortened considerably but I still love it nonetheless. Obviously, as we come to a halt and the doors open, the collective hurry and impatience projectiles us all onto the station platform. I adjust my tote bag's straps threatening to slide off my shoulder yet again as I pass through the exit barriers and take a left for my short walk to the office.

Webwise was launched only a couple of years ago by Joanna, but it's already hailed as one of the top companies in the digital agency world. Joanna and I worked together previously except, she had a ton more experience and expertise than I did but corporate politics kept her in the same position and salary bracket as me, a new-born in comparison to a wise sage-her. She took the plunge, started her own agency, poached me and brought me along for the ride and I happily obliged. I get to have my own team, work for some of the best small and big businesses and have a boss who is more of a friend, it's a pretty sweet deal to be honest.

I tap my access card and walk in through the automatic glass doors only to stop dead in my tracks as a very familiar face looks up from the lounge chair in our tiny reception.

"Oh, um, hi Teddy."

My face pales as I spit out the first conclusion my brain arrives at, "Seb are you following me?" I cry out.

"What? No! I should be asking you that, since I've already been here for ten minutes and you have just arrived."

"Not following, I meant stalking. Semantics. Don't lie Seb, have you been stalking me?"

He cracks a smile, "Wow, you haven't changed at all," he says as he shakes his head at me.

"Wha-"

"Oh wonderful, I see Thea you have met our new client," Joanna swishes into the reception area with her flared printed silk trousers and wild curly hair. "Sebastian, meet Thea. She's the best. She's helmed the most number of campaigns out of any of us here and her deliverables are basically untouchable, in quality and quantity."

Seb, who had stood up as Joanna was singing my praises (I'm not complaining), is smiling at me like a madman. Or a proud friend. I will go with option one, a madman.

"We actually know each other," Seb tells Joanna, "from university."

"Oh?" Joanna looks over at me in surprise. "Well it's settled then," she looks back at Seb, "I was going to assign you to one of my other teams but this works out well. Thea can work with you!"

What. The. Hell. This cannot be happening.

"Right, Thea? You already know him, it's a good head start-"

"I don't even know what he does!" I screech out, interrupting Joanna. They're both looking at me with wide eyes so I clear my throat and speak at a level tone.

"I mean, we haven't met in years. It actually may even be a disadvantage, you know."

"I don't see how, it could be a nice reunion!" Joanna claps her hands and looks over at Seb to agree with her considering I'm being no help to her.

"I'm fine with whatever you decide," he says to me, crossing his hands behind his back that involuntarily broadens his chest and shoulders.

I avert my gaze and ask Joanna, "Hey, can I talk to you, alone, for a second?"

She nods and we excuse ourselves from Seb and walk further into the office, stopping at an empty desk. Before I can explain the situation and plead my case, Joanna launches into her own line of questioning.

"Who is he? He is so cute, why don't you want to work with him? He seems nice, is he not nice?"

"Easy grasshopper, he is nice, I think at least but, um, we have history?"

"What kind of history?"

"Just...there is tension."

"Sexual tension?"

"JOANNA."

"What? You are being so vague, what else would I assume? Did you date? Did he reject you?"

"We did not date, no. We were just really good friends and it did not end well. Let's just say it wasn't friendly how it ended." I disregard her last question. What she doesn't need to know, she doesn't need to know.

"Ooh, drama. Look I get it, lord knows I have "friends" I wouldn't want to be friendly with either, but can you seriously consider doing this? I know I sprang this on you out of nowhere but anyone else would only be able to take him on after a few weeks if not months, and you are just finishing up that campaign for that vibrator company,"

"They are not vibrators, they are portable massagers for muscle spasms."

"Darling, you and I both know why their demographic was seventy-five percent millennials and gen z. Anyway, can you please do this for me? We have to turn away enough clients as is with our small workforce."

"Ugh…Fine." I give up and agree.

"I love you. So much. I owe you one!"

Even if I refuse to work with Seb, it's inevitable that I will see him around more often, with him being my next-door neighbour. It'll only be more awkward running into him in the future if I send him away today. And I can't sequester myself away from ever bumping into him, so may as well be a big girl about it and act professionally. Plus, a little curious part of me wants to know what he is like now. Starting with, where does he even work? What does he want a digital marketing campaign for? I follow Joanna back to Seb as she giddily approaches him. I don't blame her actually, that's the effect Seb has on everyone. Be it a young girl, an old lady, or someone in their late-thirties like Joanna. Not me anymore though, I am immune. I think.

"Would you like something to drink-"

"Thank you for doing this-"

We both start talking simultaneously as we sit down in one of the meeting rooms in the office.

"Sorry, I just wanted to thank you for this. You could have said no and it would be completely understandable," he says while ruffling his hair and looking out at the office through the glass partition "I really need all the help I can get so, thank you," he says, finally turning to look at me.

"Um yeah, it's alright," I say as I avoid his gaze and focus on starting up my laptop, even though it requires zero focus and absolutely no help from me.

Standing up, I ask him again, "Would you like something to drink, I'm going to make myself some coffee."

"Sure, coffee is good."

I walk over to our kitchenette and pull out two pods for the coffee machine. As the machine buzzes and spurts out coffee in one of the mugs, I grab the milk. As I switch the mugs and start pouring the milk, I look over at Seb. He's wearing a button-up today and has taken off his coat, which is draped over his chair. It's so similar to the one he wore on the day we first met, but clearly not the same. That coat wouldn't fit this Seb. He has grown into his features and body. He was always taller than me but now his frame makes him look even more so. He catches my eye and that is my cue to stop stirring the bean juice and get back to work.

He thanks me as I hand him his mug, "You still remember how I take my coffee?" He says after taking a sip.

I peer at his mug and notice the milky appearance. I don't know how, but in my daze, I had made him his coffee.

"It's just muscle memory I guess, I didn't even think about it," I tell him honestly and there's an almost, imperceptible fraction of sadness that comes and goes from his face. I brush this thought aside and glare at him from over my mug as I guzzle down some more of my drink. "You sure you didn't stalk me?"

He gives me a bored look, "I swear, I just googled digital marketing agencies and you guys were practically everywhere."

"And that's on good SEO, what good is a digital marketer if they can't market themselves?" I say proudly.

"Exactly, and uh, I promise I didn't stalk you but I'm glad we met. Here, and with being neighbours," his pitch increases all of a sudden, "which was also by complete chance! Had no idea you were moving in…I think fate decided before we could-"

"So I will need you to start from the beginning, what do you need us for?" I interrupt him and get into work mode. If we start this now I doubt I will be able to compartmentalise him as just a client. I can't let the lines blur even before this project takes off. "I believe you had a chat with Joanna but with how sudden this was, I haven't been able to ask her anything. I usually have some ideas prepped for a first meeting but-"

"It's okay, I understand," he immediately reassures me, probably because he thinks I would find any reason to not continue being here with him right now.

"So, this is for a new art gallery-"

"Seb," I exclaim, "you work in an art gallery?"

"Actually, I own the art gallery." He says casually, like it's no big deal. Anyone else saying that would sound smug, but not Seb. There's a quiet confidence in him. It doesn't envelope his entire persona, but slowly simmers just beneath the surface; far away from cocky and just the right amount of self-assured.

"Oh my God?" I gawk at him. "This was your dream! I can't- oh my God! Congratulations!" Whatever happened to not letting the lines blur, idiot.

"Yeah, just bought the place a few months ago. I've been finding artists for the first exhibit and getting the place ready and now there's only a month left until opening, so I need to get the word out…"

"Woah, just a month? We need to work quickly and boost this," I open a blank document and start jotting ideas that come to my mind immediately. "But, this is amazing Seb, I'm very happy for you." I am in awe, this is what we used to talk about all those years ago and he's only gone ahead and done it. I can be proud of him and not want to see his face at the same time. It's not mutually exclusive.

"Thank you, Teddy," he says, his face turning pink.

And that name pulls me back to reality. I school the expressions that had betrayed me and compose myself.

"It's Thea," I correct him and diffuse the moment.

"Right, sorry."

As we continue exchanging ideas and building a plan, I wonder when I can ask him what I have been wanting to know for six years. When will it be a good time? I don't want to hinder any work and remain strictly professional but the more time I spend with him, my exterior will only break more. I won't be able to snap in and out of the Teddy he knew and the Thea I am now if I keep pestering myself with the past. But how do I even escape it if his mere existence is my past?

"You could come to have a look at the gallery someday?" He asks hesitantly. "To get a feel of the place and see the exhibit yourself, there's only so much I can tell you and show you pictures of…"

"Yeah, sure. That would be helpful." For the digital campaign. For me? Not so much.

5

With you I'd dance in a storm

8 years ago

The London skies are adorned with dark grey clouds all over, silently warning everyone of the downpour that's going to greet us soon. Since I don't have any classes today, I would've ideally preferred to stay in my room and enjoy my own company. Maybe watch a show (binge a whole season or two), catch up on the readings for my course modules (doze off after a couple of pages) or do my laundry (I would have actually done that, my hamper is toppling over). But instead, I'm headed to the nearby bus stop after receiving a text from Seb, to meet him here for an adventure. I had replied back asking for details but he just left me on read. Classic. If there's one thing I've come to know about him, it's that he loves these impromptu excursions. His 'adventures'. Though there's hardly anything adventurous about them. And I'm grateful for that because I don't possess a single athletic bone in my body. Nor does Seb. But you wouldn't guess that by looking at his body. Not that I have seen his body body, I'm just assuming, you know. Fit people just look fit. I have eyes. Conjecture.

"Where to today, mister?" I ask as I approach his leaning figure against the pole at the bus stop.

"Hint: it rhymes with 'fate'," he answers as he interlocks his left arm with my right, that's shoved inside my coat's pocket, as he leads us away from the bus stop.

"Tate?"

"Ding-ding-ding-ding!"

"Of course, I should have guessed it before the hint." Seb's love for Tate Modern knows no bounds. And this proclivity has permeated to me by association. We don't always need new exhibits or installations to visit the famed gallery. Sometimes we just walk around seeing the things we have already seen but somehow, we always notice something new to talk about.

"Wait, why are we not taking the bus then?"

"Because we are taking the tube."

"Why?"

He shrugs looking straight ahead, "Because you like taking the tube," he says matter-of-factly.

I smile up at him even though he's not looking at me. I know he knows I appreciate this. It's just best friend telepathy.

We share a pair of earphones on our ride to Tate Modern. It's connected to his phone so he presses play on a podcast from its midway point that he must have been listening to. The hosts are discussing Rococo-era art and I can't help but let out an exaggerated fake yawn as I look at him sideways. Wordlessly he understands that going to Tate is enough art for me today. He rolls his eyes and pauses the audio, pulling his phone closer to his face to search for something (hopefully) more interesting. As I'm looking around assessing our carriage and trying to discern which side the gates will open at our station, an unfamiliar tune fills my ear. I look over at him and he's deliberately avoiding my eyes, feigning interest in the map overhead, with a cheeky smile threatening to break out on his face any second. The singer in our ears has started singing words over the melody but I still don't recognise the song. I take Seb's phone and touch the screen to wake it up. 'An Art Gallery Could Never Be As Unique As You' by the artist mrld.

"They should revoke your access to any and all art galleries in London for that," I whisper to him as I shake my head, "some aficionado you are."

"Excuse me, I was happy with my podcast. That's called dedicating a song to your best friend, you unappreciative creature."

The train halts at our stop and we get out of the station, heading towards Southbank.

"I see who you are Seb, I see it," I say as I squint my eyes at him, "what would the love of your life, art, say when it finds out your loyalties are dwindling?"

"Shut up, you're too sceptical for your own good," he chuckles and ruffles the top of my hair.

"Yeah yeah, now let me dedicate a song to you." I press play on Bad Liar by Selena Gomez as we near the entrance of Tate Modern.

Entering the Turbine Hall at Tate Modern never gets old. The sloping entrance, the sheer height of the space, families, couples, children, friends lounging around the steps on the side.

"So, I wanted to come here today for this new Jenny Holzer exhibit," Seb says as we take the escalators. "She's an American artist, her work basically revolves around words."

"Words?"

"Yeah, like sentences, or statements, in different forms. Neon lights, ticker signs, etched on marble benches, stuff like that. But the focus is on her words. One of her pieces, Truisms, is 300-something sayings and adages. Stuff we all have seen and know but all in one place, one after the other. It's all so powerful and provocative in its simplicity."

"Wow," I am stunned, "I actually can't wait to see it now. Not gonna lie, the Rococo podcast made me think I would be looking at paintings of people lounging in their gardens and dancing in nature."

"Another time."

"I'm sure."

As we enter the first room of the exhibit, I instantly realise what Seb was talking about. All four walls of the small room are covered in words. Sentences. Each is self-sufficient with no conjunctions joining one to another. They all exist on their own, but seeing it all at once is daunting and takes a life of its own. It's impossible but it makes you want to stand and read each and every one of them. They are simple in their meaning but it is a wondrous thing to behold. In my peripheral view, I can already see a glimpse of the next room and the neon lights Seb was talking about. We are both taking our time reading the words quietly. If one of us wants the other to see the same sentence they are reading, all we have to do is just look at them and point to where the words are. The acknowledgement is a nod or a simple "Yes, that's a good one" or some iteration of the same.

We slowly make our way to the other rooms of the exhibit together. Circling around each other and crossing tracks, back to back or in two separate corners, but together. Usually, when the exhibit has paintings or sculptures, we move in tandem and discuss the meaning, the intentions, the context, the talent or whatever the art reminds us of. Today, there is an implicit understanding that we don't need to use our words. The art is doing the talking today. We reach the part of the exhibit where the installation comprises small, rectangular, black metal plaques hung on walls, inscribed with even more of Jenny Holzer's words. Halfway through the first wall, one of the plaques catches my attention and I stop to read it over and over. "People look like they are dancing before they love."

"That's beautiful," I get startled as Seb comes up behind me, "Sorry, didn't mean to scare you."

"It's okay, I was so fixated on this one I forgot where I was for a second, it is beautiful, it reminded me of my parents."

"Your…parents?" Seb inquiries with disbelief.

"Yeah, before my dad left us obviously. Years before that," I explain as we stand there looking at the plaque. "When my sister and I were babies. I must have been around 5, and Millie, 2. Long before we could understand adults and their feelings, I remember one night Dad putting on some old song and pulling my mom up from the couch, twirling her around, as they both waltzed and laughed into each other's shoulders. They were too tall for us, naturally, so Millie and I just clung to their legs and then danced on our own when they moved too much for us. And it was just so, happy." I start walking as I reminisce and Seb keeps up beside me. "They looked so in love, even in my memory, after everything I know now, they still look like they were each other's world, you know? I don't know if I'm just latching onto what I thought I knew then. It must be the age right? When you are 5, 6, 7? Your parents are everything. They are it. You think they know everything, they can do anything, they are invincible. And most importantly, they belong together. Mom with Dad and Dad with Mom. You see them as one entity rather than two individuals who have chosen to be together, because you don't know any other reality than that. Only to one day be 10 years old and realise nothing was as it seemed. Dad had been pretending, he wasn't happy and he couldn't do it anymore." I say mournfully as we reach the ground floor where we had started.

"You know Mom says it was over between them much before he left," we manoeuvre the crowd of people trying to make their way inside the building as we head out. "I don't get why he couldn't just leave before? Why give us this false sense of a complete and happy family, years worth of good memories, only to tarnish them one day, out of the blue? I keep looking back at every piece of my childhood, trying to discern whether it was real or an act, clouding my judgement. I have no idea how I should feel every time I remember a memory. He should have just left the minute he knew he was done."

"I'm sorry, that must be the absolute worst," I shrug as we stop in front of the railing overlooking the Thames river, "buuut," I look over at him questioningly as he throws his hands up.

"Not defending your dad but, maybe he was just trying and failing at trying." I gesture at him to elaborate.

"See, I don't think he would have wanted to inflict pain deliberately on you, your sister or even your mom. You have happy memories with him then just take them for what they are. Don't over analyse it, maybe he just… cared?" he tilts his head as if trying to make sense of it himself. "He cared and he was trying. He didn't leave earlier because, maybe he didn't want to give up so easily. He kept showing up until his unhappiness, or whatever he was going through, got bigger than his efforts. You can never tell what it looks like when someone is trying. It's different for everyone." I hum as we both look at the water lapping at the wall below. Seb adds, "Still very shitty of him so you don't have to forgive him or anything, but you don't have to resent your memories either. They are yours, no one else can have a hold over them."

I look at him as tiny droplets begin to fall from the sky, "You should be a therapist."

He rolls his eyes and looks up at the clouds, "I'm serious, that was very wise advice."

"Well you're welcome, it's the least I can do for your future abandonment issues."

"Don't say that and will it into existence, please."

"Oops, sorry."

It is now beginning to rain with its full might and I begin to power-walk towards one of the shops to take cover.

"Teddy! Wait!"

"What? Come on, the rain's getting worse-"

Seb grabs one of my hands and stops me from running. I raise my eyebrows as I turn to look at him. He reaches into his pocket to retrieve his phone, which is surely not going to survive this bath. I can't make out what he is doing on the screen as rain droplets blur my vision by clinging onto my eyelashes. Suddenly, I hear music playing. Seb smiles at me as he raises our intertwined hands to twirl me around once, then twice and thrice. Giggling and trying to find my balance, I steady myself as he softly says, "Here's to making new dancing memories."

I smile up at him, because I know he knows what I want to say. Best friend telepathy.

6

Why are we pretending this is nothing

Present day

I had a meeting ten minutes from Seb's gallery, so after trying to forget about his invitation for two whole days, I decide it was about time. The two of us made a groupchat with my team and his employees so we could keep everyone in the loop regarding the work we do, but is paying a visit to his gallery something everyone needs to be intimated of? Technically, it's for work, he said it would help me ideate the campaign better, so I could just shoot a text on the group, no big deal. But also, it's him and, it's me, I should text him privately, ask if he's busy. Ugh, why am I overthinking this? I act on impulse and tap on his number to start a separate conversation. Within seconds he has read my text and a reply comes in saying I could drop by anytime, he's free. I leave the building I had my meeting in and start towards his gallery.

It's weird seeing a brand new text thread with Seb when we have had years worth of conversations on text before. I mean, it's better this way, not having to confront how close we once were. He told me he had a new number now, before he proceeded to recite it for me to save on my phone. I wonder if he knows how acutely aware of this I was already, given how he had stopped replying and checking that number the day after his graduation. How if I hadn't deleted our chat a year after he left, or if he had still kept his old number, the last evidence of our friendship would have been one-sided consecutive texts from me, asking where he was, was he okay, was he off an an 'adventure' without telling me, I would even accept a read receipt if he didn't want to reply, how I was slowly getting angry, then sad, asking if I had done something wrong, if I was at fault then I was sorry, accepting that it must be me, denying how it could even be me, thinking it was an elaborate joke and claiming I had caught on, pleading for my best friend to come back because I was so alone, angry voice notes from drunk nights when I spiralled and finally, a few weeks of silent treatment and then a lone goodbye. I had kept that thread archived for a few months, hoping that keeping proof of my efforts would somehow give me answers, despite his number being out of service for months at the time. Finally, I deleted the chat, thinking it would act as closure, only to scramble back to my phone, cursing myself and trying to undo my actions to no avail. So yeah, Seb, I know it's a new number.

The map on my phone alerts me that I have reached my destination. I look up and find it, right off the main street that I have been walking on, inside a gated compound. It's quite centrally located and easily visible for anyone trying to look for it for the first time, yet feels secluded and spacious enough for a gallery, due to the empty space in front of the building as you enter the compound. On days with good weather, especially during summers, he could have installations in his front yard too, much like Tate Modern. I'm certain this would have made the space so much more lucrative when he was looking for places.

The sign for the gallery has not been put up yet, kept on the side of the building wrapped in plastic, but as I approach the entry I notice a smaller sign on the wall next to the door with the name. Clean Slate Gallery. It's a sharp and clean font, white on a black background. I had seen the name on the agreement we had made for them and even the logo in the information packet his team had mailed us. But seeing it here, in real life, in front of the building that is Clean Slate Gallery, fills me up with a feeling I can't describe. I am happy and proud, yes, but it's this swirling commotion in my tummy. He has achieved it, and I wasn't there to witness it. I don't know why he chose this name or which places he had shortlisted. I don't know what he has been doing to save up enough to be able to pursue this, or if he has taken a loan. He had to have taken a loan- my phone starts ringing just as Seb appears on the other side of the glass door. I mouth "One moment" and show my ringing phone to him.

It's Millie. Damn it, I was supposed to call her this time. I back away from the door and walk into the front yard as I pick up her call.

"I'm sorry, I'm sorry, I know it was my turn to call, how are you?"

"It's fine, it's cool, not like your little sister is housebound, heavily pregnant and the sole focus of a helicopter mom who will give her unabashed, unsolicited opinion on every, fucking, thing. Mom traum is at an all-time high sissy!"

Millie got married last year and is ready to pop any day now. Growing up, we were never close and our parents didn't help our case either. My mother was obsessed with turning me into a miniature version of herself (a high-octane, social-climbing, STEM wizard), unfortunately for her, I possessed none of her brand of boss woman genes. So, her sights were set on Millie, and she delivered. Our mom got her favourite child and yet, she raised us not as siblings, but adversaries. Despite our difference in age, every task became a battle and every achievement became a competition. I don't think Millie and I resented each other much, but with Mom's games, we never saw eye to eye either. Until I left home, and then three years later Millie left too. We finally got the chance to bond and become friends and actually get to know one another. We make sure to take turns and call each other, for life updates, sharing our new favourite purchases, her love life (now a married one), my love life (or lack thereof), everything in between, but mostly for some 'mom traum' time. Aka what new mom schtick she is inflicting on us currently.

"I feel bad for you, honestly, I do but I have to say, ever since you told us you were preggers, she is so preoccupied with you that she has almost forgotten about me. So, thank you."

"This is so unfair!" She cried out like an actual baby. "And what have you been so busy with, now that you have all this free time not having to deal with mommy dearest?"

I don't want to tell her about the reappearance of a certain someone in my life. She knows the Seb lore obviously. In fact, she is the only person who knows every single thing about that phase of my life. I think sharing all that with her back then was part of the reason why we grew so close, so quickly. But, she always romanticised our friendship. I would like to believe in meet-cutes, stars aligning, divine timing and such, but not with him. Not after all these years. But if Millie comes to know about him now, I will be subjected to non-stop monologues about fate and serendipity. And so, ignorance is bliss.

"Just work. So much work. Listen, I really want to know what Mom did and actual info about your health but I have to go in for a meeting with a client right now, I'll call you tonight?"

"Oh god, yes, go! I'm fine, talk to you soon."

We say our goodbyes and I turn to go inside when I notice, Seb is still standing where he was. I'm sure he did a quick turn and started talking to the woman next to him as soon as I turned back around. Huh.

"Hi!" Seb chirps with a toothy grin like a kid being caught with contraband cookies, as I enter the gallery.

"Hi, sorry for that, it was urgent."

"No worries, a client?"

"No," shit, I denied that too fast, why didn't I just say yes? He doesn't need to be updated on my relationship with my sister. "An…associate." Sure, Millie is an associate.

"Riiight," he says with a lilt in his voice. Great, he knows I'm lying. "Anyway, let me introduce you to my associates." Asshole.

It's a small group and everyone is sweet. I recognize their names from the group chat and it's nice to be able to put faces to names. The woman Seb was talking to earlier, Jess, seems to be my age and will be handling the gallery's social channels; I easily strike up a conversation with her since our jobs are aligned and basically symbiotic. I can feel Seb standing behind me, too polite to break us up but Jess notices him rocking back and forth on his feet and apologises.

"I'm holding you up, you should probably tour the gallery," she says looking between me and Seb.

"You don't have to leave, you can join us!" I say way too excitedly, in lieu of saying please don't let me walk around a gallery alone with Seb. Jess looks over at Seb who is as civil and courteous as ever.

"Of course, it will be more efficient than exchanging emails later." That is true, that is exactly why Jess should third-wheel us. Or Seb should be the third-wheel to Jess and me.

It's a sizable place, starting with a straight, long hallway, ending with a left-turn that leads to an adjoining room, followed by two more interconnected rooms, which leads you back to the hallway where you started. There's a flow to the space that lends to a true gallery-feel. It could work with a multi-artist set-up, the way it is configured right now or also be entirely dedicated to a single artist, showcasing multiple pieces of work and helping them tell a story. You can tell it was designed with thought and care.

My curiosity gets the better of me and I ask no one in particular, "Did the place come as is or did an architect work on it?"

Seb turns around as he is a little ahead of us but Jess is closer to me so she replies, "Oh no! All credit goes to Sebastian, this gallery is his baby, he was so pedantic about everything. It's all him."

"It's really beautifully designed," I tell him in all sincerity.

"Thank you," he blushes. "Uh, so this is the last area. The hallway and the other two rooms were dedicated to an artist each but this one is a mixed bag. I wanted to curate pieces by a bunch of smaller artists who wouldn't normally get to showcase their work in a gallery setting. It's experimental but I hope people like it."

"That's a great initiative, and it looks brilliant."

Jess adds, "Everything is handpicked by Sebastian, of course." I wonder why she is wing-manning him so hard when I realise he's her boss. Go get that raise girl.

I spot a painting I like and walk towards it, Seb and Jess in tow. Oil on canvas, painted five years ago. It's a scene of a garden as a girl in a dress spins around in the centre. There are people around, minding their own business, and she's just in her own world amidst everything.

"It's a good one, right?" Jess asks me.

"Yeah, it's gorgeous."

"Well, it is made by a very talented artist, he-"

"Jess, did you see the email I had sent you this morning?" Seb interrupts Jess, which is very unlike him. Both Jess and I are looking at him with pinched brows. Well, must be an important email.

"I think so? I will check it again, I can't seem to recall."

"Yes please, whenever you get the time," Seb clears his throat.

Jess nods vehemently as she returns back to my side, "You should buy this one, once we open to the public," she resumes her focus on the canvas.

"Ah, I don't know about that, Mac wouldn't be too fond of the dogs in the foreground." Machiavelli would hiss at the painting endlessly if he noticed the pet dogs in it.

"Mac?" Jess asks as I feel Seb's eyes on me.

"My roommate." I don't know why I say that, I don't know why I choose this ambiguous answer instead of a simple three-letter word called cat.

"I didn't know you had a roommate," Sebs states, tight-lipped, with a furrow in his brow.

Maybe I do know why I said that.

7

I don't like a gold rush

7 years ago

I don't know why but I decided that Seb and I needed to go to a party today. A girl in one of my marketing modules was having a party at her place and had sent an open-to-all invitation on the Facebook group. I have talked to her a few times and she lives close by, so why not? This is so unlike me, but this is what they say uni life is about right? New experiences and all that. This is not Seb's idea of fun either. Neither of us are party people, we didn't attend a single freshers week party and nor are we the kind to bar-hop and get drunk. But something in me wants to be someone else other than me today. Maybe it's the fact that my mom called today and interrogated me about joining so and so societies because someone's son and someone's daughter is a member and those kinds of connections would be fortunately convenient.

So not only am I not joining any societies or clubs, I'm doubling down by being rebellious and going out on a school night. There is literally no way for Mom to find out I'm doing this unless I shove pictorial evidence in her face, but this is less about making her mad and more about trying to get out of my shell in my own way and on my own terms. It doesn't matter if I come out the other side with zero takeaways because at least I would have tried. Seb, on the other hand, doesn't need to try. At all. And it's so frustrating. I spent the whole day choosing this outfit, carefully applying makeup after watching hours of YouTube tutorials and wearing heels, whereas he got back from his classes an hour ago and now he's here in a black button-up, looking effortlessly cool. With his dark curls falling into place no matter how much he fidgets with them, trying to get them out of his eyes.

"Teddy, you look…wow. I don't know what to say."

"Please, this is the most basic thing ever," I say, looking down at my black dress and tights (the fleece-lines ones!) "I don't think I have put in half the effort all these other girls have."

"Learn to take a compliment Teddy, you look amazing."

"You're just saying that mister every girl in a ten feet radius is checking me out."

"Teddy, if you're jealous you can just say that."

"Seb, PLEASE. If anything I am checking all those girls out wondering how their pores are non-existent and the wings of their eyeliner even," I say as we both scoff at each other. "Wait, there's the girl whose party this is, I should go say hi." I steer my way around the people dancing and chatting, carefully avoiding anyone's cup of booze from bumping into me.

"Oh my god, Theadora! You came!" She screams as she stumbles her way to come and hug me. "I didn't think this was your scene dude," she keeps yelling even though her face is right next to mine and the music is nearly not loud enough to occlude our hearing. She's clearly tipsy and we aren't buddies so I just give her the easiest answer.

"Of course, I had to come, it's your party after all!" God, I sound like my mother. I choose to do one thing antithetical to her and end up eerily close to her. Oscar Wilde was onto something when he wrote, "All women become like their mothers. That is their tragedy."

"Awww you're a sweetie!"

Before I can detach myself from her tight embrace and go back to Seb, another girl joins in and starts talking to us. I don't know her but oddly, she seems to recognise me.

"I have seen you around campus!" Great, she has an affinity for yelling her words too.

"Oh? In the library or-"

"I know!!! You are always with your boyfriend! I am so jelly, you two make such a cute couple," this new girl says with half-closed eyes, with her hands clasped against her chest.

"B-boyfriend? I don't have a…boyfriend?" I end up asking instead of telling her.

"Yeah you dooo, tall, curly hair, always looks cosy, doesn't leave your side because honestly, I don't think I have seen him around without you. Trust me, I would have noticed," she says with a wink.

Seb. She's talking about Seb. Is that how we look to a passing, uninformed stranger? I am struck by this revelation because it's so far from our reality. I have never even considered that as a possibility but now I'm wondering if I should? This is probably the single cup of vodka cranberry that I've consumed fogging my critical thinking.

"He's not my boyfriend," I clarify to her, "we are just friends. Best friends."

She looks at me in disbelief, her mouth opening exaggeratedly. "No way! Are you sure? You two seem pretty tight. Wait, so does that mean," she pauses to look around and whispers conspiratorially, "he is single?"

I am once again taken aback. I have literally tried to set him up with girls we see around, why is this question being directed at me feel like an attack. I shake this feeling away by physically shaking my head.

"Yeah, he's single."

"Awesome! You wouldn't mind if I go talk to him right?"

"No not at all, seriously, I'm not his girlfriend." I smile at the girl as she gives me an air kiss and all but skips her way towards Seb.

I shouldn't feel anything seeing them together, I could go up to anyone else here and make new friends or maybe just make small talk. But I can't seem to take my eyes away from them. They are laughing about something and my eyes shift focus from the two of them together to just Seb. He is leaning against a doorframe and the girl puts her hand on his bicep. My stomach drops at the thought of him choosing to hang out with someone else from this point on. I don't believe I am too insecure. Just like anyone else my age, I have my moments but I'm pretty secure in myself. I think. But right now, I would be lying if I said I wasn't seeing green. It wasn't so much who he was specifically talking to or that he was having a good time with someone, but rather a nagging thought in my head, that I was replaceable. After all, he never chose to talk to me in the first place, right? He just ended up next to me in a crowded hall the first day and stuck around. I was convenient, I am convenient. He could cut me out of his life and have his pick of new friends to choose from. Me, on the other hand? Who would I have?

A part of me can tell this is a detrimental spiral to go down. But the devil on my shoulder keeps coaxing me and fuelling these thoughts, forcing me to not avert my gaze from Seb. I will myself out of this weird trance and head to the table with the myriad of alcohol selections. Our host of the evening is mixing herself a drink when she spots me.

"Omg can I make you a drink, no one lets me make them a drink!" That seems like a warning in plain sight but against my better judgement, I ignore it. Bad call number one.

"Uh, sure!"

"Do you like anything in particular?" I don't even know half the bottles here, let alone trying to pick a favourite.

"Whatever's strongest." Bad call number two.

"That's what I like to hear!"

I lose count of how many liquids she is combining together. My only respite is that whatever she is pouring into my cup, she is pouring into hers too. If I am going down at least I'll have company. Though, I'm pretty sure she is a veteran in this department and immune to whatever happens after. She hands me my paper cup with the dubious concoction that has taken an almost radioactive orange colour. We clink our cups and she downs hers in a few gulps. I take a sip and almost gag from the taste, leaving me no choice but to gulp it all down too. Bad call number three. Someone then passes along shots of a clear liquid and I am given one too. Well, here's to nothing. The liquid burns my throat. Straight vodka. I grab the first bottle that I can reach and try to chase away the burning sensation with what turns out to be some IPA. Bad call number 4.

My vision starts blurring and my body loosens up soon after. I don't know who I danced with or how long I danced for. I just know I was laughing a lot. And then I was crying. No one seemed to care though, I doubt anyone there could even differentiate between tears and sweat. I start swaying on my own accord and keep having to hold on to someone or something to stay upright. My clothes feel too tight and my face feels grimy, I want to get out of here. Walking a few steps to the main door feels like an eternity as my legs weigh me down, but I make it. I am alert enough to realise that I should not head out to the streets or try and take public transport by myself at this hour, in this state. So after a few flights of stairs, I sit down and tuck my head between my knees. I didn't see Seb leave so he must still be upstairs. But I don't want to disturb him and his girl. Plus, if I try to climb these steps back up, I might throw up on myself.

"Teddy? Teddy?" I hear a distant voice call out. I want to reply but I really can't concentrate enough to know if I'm hearing this or if someone's actually saying my name.

"Shit, pick up your phone Teddy," I can make out the hurried footsteps getting closer to me so I look up, "Teddy! Oh my god, I was so scared! You can't just leave like that."

Seb comes over to sit next to me and hugs me. It's not a tight hug like the girl at the party, that was borderline choking. This is comforting, it feels nice.

"Teddy, you should have told me if you wanted to leave, one minute you were dancing and the next I didn't know where you were," he huffs out, still holding onto my shoulders with one hand.

"Sorry, I didn't want to cockblock you."

He looks me straight in the eye and laughs out loud, "God, Teddy, you should have! That was possibly the most boring conversation I have had to endure. And I go to classes with a bunch of art nerds," he starts gently stroking my back, "Plus, she wasn't you. I would have joined you instead, looked like you were having fun."

"I was having the worst time. I am never drinking again. Don't ever let me drink again."

"Got it. Now do you feel like getting up, should we get you home?"

"Yes, please. Wait!"

"Hmm?"

"Seb?"

"Teddy."

"Promise I will always be your best friend and you will be mine. You cannot ever leave me."

"With your abandonment issues, no chance," he chuckles.

"I'm serious," I say with as much sobriety as I can muss up and open my droopy eyes as wide as I can.

"I promise, Teddy," he says with a nod.

"Good. Now please let's get out of here."

"Yes ma'am."

8

The greatest loves of all time are over now

Present day

Feeling a bit under the weather, I have decided to work from home today. With pollen season in full swing, my constant cough attacks are abysmal. I wouldn't want to distract my co-workers, hacking violently every few minutes. Apart from obviously not wanting them to contract hay fever too. Not like I could go into the office even if I wanted to, ever so pristine Joanna would take one look at my dishevelled appearance and banish me from her vicinity. Machiavelli and I are sitting at the bay window, in opposing corners. An unspoken agreement that if you don't cough on me I won't sit on your keypad, send keysmash emails to all your contacts and walk away from the crime scene, licking my paws. Because that has totally never happened before. Completely unheard of, hypothetical incident.

I feel my throat itch, the precursor to another round of coughing as Mac looks up at me, as if he has had a premonition of what's about to happen. Right as I begin coughing, there is a succession of knocks on the door. The combination of two scares poor Mac as he jumps up and dashes straight across from the bay window, pushing over the pot of Peace Lilies on my centre table, resulting in a crashing sound as the terracotta pot breaks into tiny pieces and the soil goes all over my carpet and floor. What a glorious start to my day, I think to myself, still coughing, as I avoid the mess and go to open the door.

"Thea, are you okay?"

I'm not, but why is he asking me that? Also, he was home? How did I not hear anything through our otherwise flimsy wall?

"You have been coughing up a storm all morning." Ah, that makes sense. How could I hear anyone else when I have been the wailing banshee all along.

"It's the pollen," I murmur, not to aggravate another coughing fit by using my voice too much. "Sorry if it's been disturbing, I didn't realise you would be home."

"A little coughing is not a disturbance Thea, I just wanted to know if you needed anything," he says out of genuine concern. "I have to work out some logistics and admin stuff so I'll be home all day, if you need something."

"Thanks Seb, I'm good though."

He sighs and I notice his eyes lower from mine and fix on something behind me on the floor. I follow his line of sight and look at the scattered Peace Lilies. The Peace Lilies he gifted me.

"I mean if you didn't like them you could have just given it back to me," he smirks, "or maybe it's better this way, channel your anger on the plant so I don't have to bear the brunt of it."

This is the first time either one of us has acknowledged the repercussion of our shared history. Me being me, I ignore it and defend myself to him instead.

"I didn't do it! It was Mac, he got scared and ran past it, knocking it over. Ugh, I'll have to re-pot it now."

"Your roommate? Ran past it?" He asks, voice laced with confusion as he tilts his head to the side.

"It's a cat Seb, my roommate's a cat," I open the door further, letting Seb decide if he wants to step in as I go and retrieve my feral feline from the kitchen counter.

"Meet Machiavelli," I take him to Seb, who has crossed the threshold but did not dare to come in any further.

"No wonder."

"What?"

"Oh that day in the gallery when you told us, I was wondering how much of a douchebag your roommate was, if he couldn't even help you haul all those boxes the day you were moving in. Well, now it makes sense why he couldn't."

Seb strokes under Mac's chin, which makes him purr. Though as soon as he stops, he leaps out of my hands and lands directly on the Peace Lilies. He looks straight into Sebs eyes as he tears a flower apart with his nails, he moves onto another flower while still staring at Seb. It is kind of intimidating and I feel a sort of kinship I have never felt with an animal before.

"So, I won't have to re-pot that now."

"You got a pet cat," Seb says, point-blank.

"You got a gallery," I say with a smile.

He shrugs a single shoulder and looks away.

"Listen, about that. You have worked so hard on the marketing-"

"It's my job, you're paying me."

"Yeah, but you did work hard, we are almost fully booked for the opening week with the ticket sales from your ads. It's only fair that you come to the opening night. I would really like for you to be there…"

I ponder over his invitation. I would love to see his gallery come to life. I got a sneak peek before but to witness it, as a part of a crowd, would be something else. But something's stopping me. It feels like I am stuck in quicksand. The more I try to get out of it, the deeper it pulls me in. This is like opening a wound deliberately to feel the pain again, for no rhyme or reason. Like when you play a game you used to love as a child, you throw away the instruction manual thinking 'I got this', but you don't. You have forgotten the why's and the how's and now you're looking it up online to make some sense of it. After all these years, we were back on square one but this feels like skipping a lot of the steps and trying to pick up where we left off.

"I'll think about it."

He nods, "Let me know. And I'm here if you need me."

I look at him quizzically.

"For the coughs. If it gets worse and you need anything."

"Yes, of course."

He takes his leave and after shutting the door, I stand over my ruined carpet, wondering how to salvage it. A blunt knock directs my attention to the wall. Did Seb knock something over too? I hear a couple of knocks again, and it sounds deliberate. I go over to our shared wall and knock back twice, the same way he did. He knocks once again and I leave it at that.

I don't know what it means. He never taught me morse code, only BSL. I'm in half a mind to Google if it means anything but I stop myself. It doesn't matter. It doesn't matter because not everything he does has an ulterior motive. Sometimes, if it looks like a duck, swims like a duck and quacks like a duck, then it probably is a duck. It's just a reminder that he is here. A knock back once more and he reverts back instantly. Yeah, he is here.

9

Confess my truth in swooping, sloping, cursive letters

7 years ago

So, we are in Paris. Last evening, we were lounging around Seb's flat when he was telling me about all the museums in France. It's reading week and Seb's adventure bug has surely caught me because I was the one to suggest we take a day trip to Paris. Seb thought I was joking until I pulled up his laptop and started looking up Eurostar tickets for the next morning. We have both saved up from our part-time jobs, it's only fair that those savings get to see the light of day. Lights of the Eiffel Tower, specifically.

And that is how we ended up in Paris. We have already toured Musée d'Orsay, Musée de l'Orangerie and the Rodin Museum. We did go to the Louvre but it's too big to tackle in a few hours, so we said a quick hello to Mona Lisa and headed to the Dalí museum in Montmartre. Currently, trekking up the steep steps of the area to reach the top, where the museum is located.

"Hurry up! We have to come back down in time too, to catch the Montmartre tour," Seb says nonchalantly. I curse him under my breath for having better-functioning lungs than me.

"I hope Salvador Dalí is appreciating the struggle I'm enduring to see his work. Seb, this is torture."

"No, you are just being a baby."

"Yes, I am a baby, carry me."

Seb actually walks down to me and in one swoop, proceeds to lift me, bridal style, and continues climbing the steps like my weight is equivalent to that of a feather.

"Oh my God!"

"Kind of you to call me that but I still prefer Seb."

I slap him on his chest, "Shut up and put me down, I was joking!" I whisper-yell at him as I notice everyone around looking at us and smiling a knowing smile. "People are looking!"

"Who cares, we are almost there."

A final sprint (yes, an actual sprint, on the stairs, while carrying me) later, we finally reach the top and Seb carefully puts me down.

"I can't believe you just did that."

"I can't believe that you won't believe that I will always take your words seriously."

I shake my head and wave him aside as we try to find the museum.

As we stepped inside, we fell back into our routine of observing and admiring pieces together. With Seb being in his final year, he knows a lot more now than he did when we first started visiting museums together. Who needs those guided audio tours when you have Seb giving you live commentary. He tells me all about the famous painting 'The Persistence of Memory' and the many iterations of Dalí's melting clocks, a couple of which are displayed in this museum. It's almost as fascinating to listen to him, as seeing these age-old, iconic works of art themselves. There is something so magnetic about people who are so passionate about something. You see it take over their entire body. Their eyes twinkle and their face lights up, blood rushes to the apple of their cheeks as they try to fit as much of their love for this one thing in their words, as there is in their hearts. Some people like to walk around, the adrenaline compelling them to utilise this burst of energy. Then, like Seb, there are those who can't help but use their hands to gesticulate, to emphasise everything they are saying. Showing you that they truly believe in what they are sharing, and that if you step into their world for a moment, you can too.

Only passionate people can show you magic even in the mundane.

As we approach the exit, there is a wall mural full of quotes by Salvador Dalí. There are the classics- "I don't do drugs. I am drugs.", "I enjoy cuckolding modern art.", and right at the top is one I have never seen before. "My most beautiful memories are those of the future." I don't think there could be a better quote to describe how I feel with Seb. No matter how much fun I have with him today, it's only going to get better tomorrow. As if we are always on the precipice of something bigger and better when we are with each other.

"Uh oh," Seb looks at the time on his phone, "we only have five minutes until the Montmartre walking tour starts below."

"It's okay, we don't have to do everything, right? Let's leave something for next time," I reassure him.

"Teddy, I think this is a good time to tell you that regardless of if we join them or not, they have my card blocked and will take the money anyway."

"Oh, hell no!"

I grab his hand and we get out of there as quickly as possible. Thankfully the way down to the meeting point for the tour is not all stairs but a rather long, sloping street, lined with shops with outdoor displays, restaurants with outdoor seating and multiple people going up and down.

"I think I'm going to fall," I say as the slope makes me involuntarily gain momentum. The wind is blowing against us as we dodge all the pedestrians and inanimate objects.

"3 minutes Teddy! RUN!"

I trust Seb as we both take off, being reflexively guided by our feet. We are running, so carefree that it feels like we are flying. Laughing uncontrollably as we pass by the world, just the two of us. The gush of wind in our eyes is making us cry but we don't really care. I let go of all my inhibitions at that moment. Letting my feet take over, not caring if I slipped or tripped as long as I could feel the wind blowing against me, as long as I felt this free. Mid-run Seb somehow catches hold of my hand and we are linked for the rest of our mad dash. Even then he somehow manages to point at a flower stall we pass and declare, "I would have bought you that bunch of roses, if we had more time here."

"Valid excuse."

We giggle and keep running downhill, like children who just live in the moment, not worried about what comes next. As the end of the sloped road comes into sight, we slow down and take a beat to catch our breath, from all the running and cry-laughing.

"Made it, with seconds to spare! Only us Teddy, only us!" He exclaims as he pulls me closer on that street in Paris, in front of Moulin Rouge, and twirls me around. And I think every birthday candle, shooting star and stray eyelash has led me here. And I think that's when I knew I had fallen in love.

10

I'll be getting over you my whole life

7 years ago

I don't know how I've only realised this a couple of months ago, but now that I know, it makes complete sense. I love Seb. It's unreal to think that I have thought this so many times over the past two years, even said it to him in passing, but this time, it means something completely different. It means so much more. And I have decided I will tell him how I feel after his graduation ceremony today. For once, I'm trying not to get all in my head about what he will say, if he feels the same way or if I'm going to be making a complete fool of myself. It's okay, because he's my best friend. I have nothing to be scared of.

I would have gathered the courage to tell him after our Paris escapade but we have not been spending as much time together with it being the last few months of his final year. He would have had a ton of deadlines to meet and exams to prepare for, so I've been giving him space too. All in good time.

We have been texting back and forth since morning, trying to coordinate the time and place to meet before the ceremony starts. His tone from his texts come across different than usual, more subdued, but I brush it aside blaming my own nerves and heightened anxiety. I reach the auditorium earlier than we had planned and waited for him to arrive with his parents. Even though everyone graduating looks the same today, donning the same cap and gown, something about Seb stands out. I notice him walking towards me instantly, parting the crowd as he did the first day we met. I meet him halfway and give him a hug.

"Congratulations!" My voice is muffled against his collarbone. "I'm so proud of you!"

"Hold your horses Teddy, haven't received the piece of paper yet," he laughs.

I notice his parents looking over at us fondly and part with him to greet them.

"Mum, Dad, this is Teddy." I elbow him on the side. "Sorry, this is Theadora."

"It's so lovely to meet you honey," his mom comes over to give me a hug, "we've heard so much about you."

"Likewise, it's so nice to meet you both," I say as I shake hands with his dad.

I see where Seb gets his looks from, I see where he gets any and everything from. His parents are so charming, and you can tell they dote on him. We haven't discussed our plans post-ceremony but I hope I can spend some more time with them. Seb and his dad notice his mom getting emotional and comfort her. Through her tears, she tells me, "Thank you for being such a good friend to him dear, for taking care of him."

"Of course, if anything I think he was the one taking care of me most of the time."

That felt odd for graduation day. I know parents get emotional but that was…a bit much? I don't know. I don't have a good reference point to relate to since my mother is far from emotional and much too detached to cry for my well-being. And Seb's an only child, this must be a big deal for them as a family.

Before it's time to enter the auditorium, I help them get pictures and click some for some of the other families around us too. His parents go in to take their seats first so it's just me and Seb outside. I contemplate if I should tell him my confession now but decide against it. This is his moment to shine, I don't want him to be thinking of anything else as he closes this chapter of his life. He looks at me for a long time before coming in for another hug.

"You're extraordinary," I tell him.

"You're…" he let's go to look at me once again, "everything."

We smile at one another as he heads inside, with one final wave. I can tell he had wanted to say something more but stopped himself. It doesn't matter, I can ask him later.

I hoot and cheer the loudest in the audience when his name gets announced and he walks across the stage. I take multiple pictures and videos in case his parents couldn't get a good shot. I watch him exit the stage and walk to the back of the room like all the other graduated students, waiting for the moment all the degrees are distributed and I can be reunited with him. Little did I know, that was the last I would see of him that day. And for years to come.

11

People are people and sometimes we change our minds

6 years ago

It's been a year and there's still no sign of him. His phone is out of service, his socials are deactivated and no one has a single clue of what happened to him. Sometimes I wonder if he was just a figment of my imagination. Sometimes I wonder if I jinxed something too good to be true.

I will be graduating today but I cannot muster up the kind of excitement I had exactly one year ago today. It's just a hollow reminder of what should have, could have been. Once I walk off that stage, I need to turn a new leaf and forget everything about him and everything that reminds me of him. Tomorrow's a new day.

12

I can't say hello to you and risk another goodbye

I need to ask Jess some questions regarding the screenshots she had sent us with the engagement statistics, since we don't see that data on our end. I am not too far from the gallery so I decide to drop in rather than starting a whole new email chain with unnecessary back and forth. Once I reach the compound, I don't even have to enter the building to look for her. She's right outside the entryway, overseeing two men putting up the main sign board that was kept to the side, the last time I was here.

"Hi, Jess!" I accidentally startle her.

"Oh hi, Thea! How are you?"

"Same old, same old, the sign looks nice," I say pointing to the flex board the men are levelling at the present.

"Yeah, doesn't it? Oh, Sebastian's not in today, so you'll have to make do with me."

"Oh no, I actually wanted to meet you, some queries from my team about the screenshots."

"Oh yeah sure, if you could just give me five-ish minutes, Sebastian has asked me to send him a picture once they're done putting this up."

"Of course, no problem, I'll wait."

We watch on as the men make adjustments and centre it right above the doorway. It looks even better than I had imagined as the black background pops out starkly against the white exterior of the structure. My curiosity gets the best of me as I wonder out loud, "Why Clean Slate?" It has been on my mind since the first time I saw the name. It's a common phrase obviously but knowing Seb, nothing is the way it is without reason.

"Because of the cancer and all that," Jess speaks up beside me.

"Huh?" What is she talking about?

"Sebastian. He had cancer, it was the Pancreas I think. The name's a tip of the hat to new beginnings and a fresh start after everything he went through. Really fitting, don't you think?"

"Yeah," I reply absentmindedly and I'm trying to process what I have just found out. "When was this, I mean, do you know, when he had…cancer?"

"I haven't asked him but it was a long time back, I think I remember someone saying it was right after university? I'm not sure."

I nod as my mind goes into a spiral. Jess asks me to come in and we sit down as she explains the screenshots to me. I don't know how I will relay any of what she said back to my team as everything she says just thrashes against me like waves hitting the shore again and again and again. There's a whirlpool brewing inside of me as the revelation makes way for the genesis of a whole new set of questions. When did he find out? Why didn't he tell me? Where was he all that time? Why couldn't he tell me? How bad was it? Was I not important enough to him to know? I berate myself for being so selfish. It's not about you, imagine what he went through. It's so asinine to think all this while I had been conjuring every possible reason as to why he had planned to intentionally hurt me. But he did hurt me anyway. Ugh. I don't know how to feel. I am angry, I am sad, I am disappointed, I feel ashamed but mostly, I just want to cry, because I'm confused. How do I even bring this up to him? Do I even bring it up?

"Is there anything else you wanted to know, Thea?" Jess' voice snaps me back to the present.

"Uh no! That's all, thank you for doing this."

"Anytime!"

I leave Clean Slate and the next thing I know I'm in the foyer in front of my flat. I don't know how I managed to reach home with the wave of emotions that are tumbling inside me right now. I put my key in to unlock the door, but don't make any movements to open the door. I look at Seb's door and realise I don't have an iota of a clue what the inside looks like. If I have not confronted him about anything yet, he hasn't tried to explain himself to me either. It's a two-way street.

13

I trace the evidence, make it make some sense

Present day

Showered, moisturised, pyjamas and hairband on, I'm in the middle of my nighttime skincare routine when there's a knock on my door. My spidey senses tell me it's Seb. Or just the fact that every time in the past month, if I hadn't been expecting a delivery and there was a knock on my door, it was Seb. But it's currently 10 PM. I really don't want to see him right now, especially with everything I have learned about him earlier today. But it's 10 PM and if he's here knocking then it must be for a good reason.

He is wearing grey sweatpants and a white t-shirt. His hair is tousled as if he has been running his hands through it repeatedly and he's wearing his reading glasses. He reminds me of a much younger Seb, digging through books and working on his laptop, trying to meet assignment deadlines. He looks so endearing and cuddly? Wait, what? I don't know what neurons my brain is firing at the moment, but this is not it.

"Seb, are you sleep-walking? You do know it's 10 in the night, right?"

"Yes Thea, I am well aware. But um,", he looks away, coursing his fingers through his hair, "I kinda have a huge favour to ask?"

"Okaaay?" I have absolutely zero guesses as to what this favour could be and it's starting to make me anxious.

"Can I sleep with you?"

"WHAT?"

"N-no that's not what I meant! Not with you, I mean can I sleep here, in your house, for the night, separately-" he word vomits.

I am seriously concerned for this man's mental health right now, "Did you see a ghost or something? Did you watch a scary movie, what is this?"

"No! Wait, I am not explaining myself properly."

"Yeah, clearly."

"Okay, so…" I lean against my door gauging that it will take some time for Seb to gather his bearings.

"What happened was, today morning I found that there was rat infestation issue in my home-"

"Woah woah woah, wait a second, are there rats at my place too?"

"No no, at least I don't think so, it was on the other side of my flat, not on this side," he says while looking at our shared wall.

"We could try to get Machiavelli to chase them out if you want. You know, cats catch rats, that should work."

"If there's anything your cat is catching, it's some sleep", he peers at Mac bundled up on his cat bed. "And no need anyway, I called the building manager and they took care of the rats and got the place fumigated."

"Okay I don't see any problems then, everything is sorted out then?"

"I thought it was, but you see whatever chemicals they used for the fumigation still hasn't cleared out of the air and it's kind of hard to stay in there without having teary eyes, let alone trying to sleep."

I look him up and down suspiciously. This seems too much of a stretch to be a lie.

"Listen, you are welcome to inspect my place yourself if you don't believe me."

I actually believe him but the creep in me wants to know what his place looks like.
"Lead the way," I motion towards his door. He rolls his eyes but unlocks it for me anyway. As the lights come

on, I immediately notice all the prints of famous paintings on his walls. Classic Seb. Other than that, there is minimal decoration and muted coloured furniture. Very classy. But he's right, a few seconds inside and my eyes and nose are wet.

"Okay, let's go back," I push him outside, trying to wipe my face with my palms. "Come on in."

After I get some tissues to dry my face, I notice Seb just standing in the middle of my living room, not knowing what to do.

"Um so, you can sleep in my room and I'll take the couch."

"Teddy, nonsense, I'm sleeping right here."

"No trust me, you really don't want to, there's cat piss on it."

He looks at my couch and then back at me, "Like, fresh cat piss?"

"Ew no, but like, it was there, once upon a time," I'm lying through my teeth, I would disown Mac the day he pissed on my couch (I really wouldn't), but I would be very angry because who knew couches were so expensive?

"And you never got it cleaned?"

Seriously can he stop this line of questioning, there is no way this six-foot-something man would be comfortable on my tiny couch.

"I did but can you just please take the bed?"

"You should take the bed," he sits down on the couch, claiming it, "that's very kind of you Teddy but I can't let a lady sleep on a couch reeking of cat piss,"

"No, you should, you had cancer!" I blurt out and immediately cover my mouth with my hand.

He's stumped and we both are simply staring at each other, wondering how to break the silence. Thankfully he takes on the responsibility before I spill anything else.

"Well, it's too late for a sympathy vote, Teddy."

"And who's fault is that?" I counter.

"Touche."

"Sorry I didn't mean-"

"No, it's alright. How did you find out anyway? Have you been stalking me?" He instantly lightens the mood and I'm grateful for that.

"I found out today itself actually, Jess told me when I asked about the gallery's name."

He nods, "You could have asked me about the gallery's name."

"You could've told me everything in the first place," I sigh and rub my eyes, "let's, let's not do this right now."

He hums in agreement and adds, "And I'm sleeping here Teddy, don't argue, please. I know you think I won't be comfortable but I'll be fine, it's just one night."

I hum in agreement like he had a second ago. I bring him extra sheets, pillows and a blanket and go to my room as he gets comfortable.

"Good night Teddy!" He shouts from the living room making me smile.

"Good night Seb, don't bother coming in here if you see any rat ghosts out there," I yell back

"No promises Ted," he chuckles.

Machiavelli meows loudly, probably telling us off for ruining his beauty sleep, but I'd like to imagine he's wishing us a good night too.

14

I can't pretend it's okay when it's not

There's a knock on the front door. Again. I wonder if I'm dreaming since Seb is right outside, sleeping in my living room. Who else could it be? I jolt awake from my sleeping state as the knocking continues. Before I can reach the door, Seb has beat me to it and opened it. There, staring wide-eyed at Seb, then me, then back at Seb, is Millie, in all her pregnant glory. I try to rack my brain if she had told me she was visiting, but I come up blank.

"You!" She bursts in and points an accusatory finger at Seb's chest. "You are Seb."

"Affirmative," he visibly gulps and then realisation dawns on him.

"Holy shit! You are Millie! Um, wow congratulations," he motions towards her bump. "The last time I saw you, it was a picture Teddy showed me from when you were sixteen? Seventeen?" He looks over at me for confirmation. "From a science quiz you had won a second-place trophy for, we found it hilarious how you were side-eyeing the boy who got first place."

"Sounds about right. Last I heard of you, you had ghosted my sister," she hisses menacingly, digging her finger deeper into his pecs. "Care to explain?"

"I had to go get cancer treatment in the Netherlands."

"Oh," she deflates and retrieves her finger in an instant, "I'm sorry to hear that."

"It was a long time ago."

Wait, that's it? This is how easy it was to find out where he had been? What had I been contemplating and scrutinising over for the past month, when all I needed was a stern visage and my pointer finger. Or maybe I just needed my little sister.

"So you two are cool now?" Seb asks, looking between us.

"And you two are hooking up now?" Millie asks, looking at our bed heads and sleepwear.

I groan as Seb begins to laugh.

"She really is your sister."

"Millie, it's not what it looks like."

"That's what they all say sissy."

I mentally face-palm myself for not telling her about the re-emergence of Seb when I had the chance to.

"No seriously, I was just crashing on the couch for the night. Long story short, fumigation. I'll go now," he picks up his phone and glasses from the table, "Thanks Teddy and don't worry, your couch is fine, no cat piss remnants to be found," he winks.

"Cat piss?" Millie says, looking at Machiavelli. "Wait, where do you live Seb?"

"Right next door," he says as he takes his leave.

"Fate." Millie fake-coughs into her hand. "What is going on in your life, why don't I know anything?" She whines as she flops down at my bay window.

"It's a long story."

"Great! Start from the beginning."

"Excuse me, first I need to know what you are doing here and how did you even come here, did you take the train?" I question her.

"I just wanted to surprise you!" She sing-songs. "And no, I'm pregnant but my logical thinking is still intact. I made Eric drive me here."

"You made your husband drive you two hours to the city, on a Saturday morning…Where is he anyway?"

"I sent him back."

"Let's circle back to your intact logical thinking-"

"Stoppp, can you please just start divulging into this Seb drama, I'm already offended that I don't know anything about this."

"I had a good reason for that, you would romanticise the shit out of it."

"Well duh, all these years later, he ends up being your next-door neighbour?"

"And my client, he says it was by complete chance, he didn't know I worked at the agency."

"AND he's your client? C'mon, it's too obvious. This is meant to be!"

"Except I still don't know why he cut me off the way he did. He called me his best friend and didn't even trust me enough to share what he was going through? Did he think I would not understand? I don't get it."

"Well, just ask him."

"It's not that easy Millie, it's taken me a month just to figure out the why and where of his disappearance."

"Wait, a month? I found that out within a minute of meeting him for the first time."

"All these emotions come rushing back every time I'm near him. Besides, it's not like he's trying to tell me his side of the story willingly anyway."

"Are you sure?"

"What do you mean?"

"What if he has been trying and you're pushing him away?" She raises a single eyebrow at me, "Knowing how evasive and non-confrontational you are-"

"Okay, feeling just a tad bit attacked."

"It's true, that is why mom still prepares fish, and you eat it, every time you visit her. You just cannot tell her that you have hated fish since you were like, thirteen."

"I don't mind it."

"But you should mind it! Why would you want to carry on with an inconvenience when you could nip it in the bud? Now jog back your memory and tell me, has he done anything that could have been remorseful or redeemable?"

"He did give me Peace Lilies as a welcome present."

"Ah, a peace offering."

"I mean they are also the most common funeral flower."

"No stop, don't do that. You have to learn to accept things at face value. Not everyone is out to get you T! I know we have the most cliched, dysfunctional upbringing, with an absent father and an overbearing mother, who messed us up and changed our brain's neural pathways for life. But just because they were shitty, doesn't mean everyone else will be too. You need to lower your defence mechanisms."

"I know, I know. I just need to work out how to broach the topic easily with him. How to not get all awkward and dumbfounded the moment I try to ask the hard-hitting questions."

"Sometimes, the only way around something is the way through it. You need to fight with him."

"What?"

"I mean it, you two need to face each other and fight it out. Stop tip-toeing around this thing, it's only making it bigger and more suffocating to live with. You need to forget about sensitivities and sensibilities and just fight with each other. Fight for each other."

"I-"

"Do you still love him?"

"It's complicated, Millie."

"No, just answer me. Don't think of circumstances or hypothetical situations or what-ifs, just say what comes to your mind."

"Yes, of course, I do."

"Then fight, for goodness' sake! You don't worry about being cordial and polite when you love someone. You don't wait for their justifications, you demand it. You show that you still care. You are the same girl who was ready to tell him that she loved him, it's not much different this time around either. "

Millie's pep talk is giving me a lot more confidence than I had imagined. I have been complacent and avoidant for long enough, it's time I resolve this thing between us, once and for all.

I hug her, or at least try the best I could to get my arms to wrap around all of her. "I think having a baby is making you wiser," I mumble against her sternum as we sit conjoined, in an awkward embrace.

"Yeah, being responsible for another human being and all that…" She sighs out.

"I actually meant that more literally, with you having two brains in your body right now."

She pushes me away with a light slap on my shoulder as we both adjust ourselves and sit upright.

"And remember, don't fight like you are on opposing sides, trying to rile the other up or one up the other. Fight like you're on the same team. You're working towards building something together, not breaking up and causing more fissures in the process."

"Okay, there's no way you are coming up with all of this therapist-speak yourself," I ask in disbelief, "you are not fooling me."

"Okay yes, that last bit was from this relationship counsellor's video I saw online BUT, the rest is all me," she announces proudly. "So now that I have injected some much-needed sense into your brain, when are you going to do it? When will you talk to him?"

"It's his gallery's opening night this evening," I ponder out loud, "but I don't want to take away this moment from him." This thought process is oddly reminiscent of the same day Millie had just brought up; the day I was going to tell him I loved him and decided against saying it before the ceremony. I can't help but think if I will somehow put a hex on today too. I go to the gallery and poof! There's no trace that he was ever there. Some of my worst nightmares over the years follow this same storyline. I meet someone and fall in love, when one random day, they decide to leave me without offering any explanation.

"Hey," she strokes my forearms, "you don't have to confront him today, or tomorrow. As long as you stay resolute and do it one of these days, you're good. But you're going to his gallery thing tonight, right?"

"Yeah, I think I will. Do you want to come along?"

"I would have loved to, but these sore feet are not walking around any gallery anytime soon."

I get changed into a maroon dress and get ready as Millie sits on my bed, feet propped up on a mountain of pillows, as she whistles and cat-calls me. As I open the door and get ready to leave, I hear a click next door and see Seb getting out of his house too. He's wearing a dark navy blue, almost dark grey sweater vest and beige trousers. The mental fortitude it takes for me to look away is too much. He notices me and freezes.

"You're coming to the gallery?" He asks me almost in disbelief.

"Yup."

"Well, you look amazing."

"Thank you. You look," handsome? Dreamy? Drool-worthy? "Great!"

"Thanks. Uh, do you want to go together, it's fine if you don't, it's just we are both heading to the same place from the same place, it makes sense-"

"Sure," I interrupt him before he starts a recital on climate change and saving the Earth, one carpool at a time.

As I'm about to shut the door, Millie shouts from my couch, "You kids have fun!"

Seb and I laugh as we bid her goodbye.

"I couldn't believe it was your sister when she burst through your door this morning," Seb starts talking as we walk to the lift. "When did you guys start talking?"

I don't know if I should bring it up but decided to be casual about it. It's only a big deal if I make it one. "Right after you left actually, not because of you but she left for uni at the same time and we realised we had more in common than we thought." He nods his head, shoving his hands into his pockets. "And, obviously bitching about mom was common ground."

He gives me a knowing look, "How is Theadora, the senior?"

"Still trying to micromanage our lives, Millie's more than mine though."

He nods as we wait in silence before the lift announces its arrival with a ding.

"So, I have a car waiting downstairs to take us," he says as we enter the lift, "but if you want I can cancel it and we could take the tube? For Old Times' Sake?"

He cares.

"I would love that."

He's been showing me that he cares.

15

Broke your heart I'll put it back together

Present day

The gallery is jam-packed and the night is in full swing. In every corner, people are raving about the space, the curation and of course, Seb. He was completely in his element and at ease here. He effortlessly chatted up with whoever came up to him and left them smiling once they were done. As one would expect, he knows the gallery like the back of his hand and moves like water between the rooms. He knows exactly which piece someone would like and guides them to it, falling into explanations and pointing out miniscule details that would otherwise go unnoticed. His love for his work pours out of him in excess, letting others subsume in the overflow.

To his guests and visitors, Seb is patient, attentive and receptive and yet somehow every time that

I have looked over at him tonight, he has been looking right back, ready to offer me a smile or a wink or a raise of his glass of champagne. I feel giddy and learning my lesson from Millie, I try not to overthink what this all means and just relish the present. Earlier, when Seb's team coaxed and guilted him into giving a speech, his eyes did not leave mine for the most part. He would look around and choose to settle back into my gaze, as if I was the anchor securing him to port, not letting him float away too far, into uncharted waters. He cracked a few jokes and as the room burst into laughter, he was only looking at me to ascertain my reaction. He didn't care if he could make the whole room laugh, it was only my reaction that mattered to him. I wonder how many such nuances I have missed, in the years that I had known him and the short while we have spent getting reacquainted now, that I simply didn't catch on and take notice of.

The night goes on and as the horde of people start thinning out, I decide to take a more serene and indulgent round of the exhibits. I have already seen everything twice over but with the groups of people situating themselves in front of the pieces for extended periods of time, I had not been able to fully immerse myself into the experience. As I continue my perusal of the main hallway, I sense a presence beside me. I don't have to look over to know what it is, we just quietly walk, and pause, and walk by the paintings in synchronicity. It's the kind of comfortable silence that only comes when you have an innate sense of familiarity with them.

He finally speaks up as we reach the second to last room, "What's the verdict?"

"I think this may be the best art gallery in London," I say matter-of-factly. " You've done it, I won't be going to any other gallery now," I say motioning generally around us at the space.

"Oof, you flatter me. You won't even visit Tate?" He gasps, placing a hand on his heart.

"Nah, you see I have an in with the owner Clean Slate, that instantly trumps every other competition," I nudge him playfully.

"Seriously though? Did you like it or are you just saying that?"

"Seb," I turn to look at him, halting our walk, "I mean it. You have worked so hard for it and it shows. In every corner of this place. It's beautiful and there is thought behind every choice. This was a huge undertaking, I can't even make sense of the kind of work that would go into building something like this from scratch. You should be proud of yourself. And so many people showed up! On your first night! That in itself is a testament to what you have created here."

"Well, that was thanks to you, if it was on me we would have had like twenty people show up."

"Ah, it was nothing."

"Don't underplay your achievements."

"First you stop doubting yourself."

We continue walking at a leisurely pace as the gallery has almost emptied out. This feels like we have stepped into a portal, time-travelling seven or eight years in the past, as we roamed and admired the exhibits at the Hayward Gallery, the White Cube, Victoria Miro, Saatchi Gallery and of course, Tate Modern. A slideshow of all those times interplay in my mind as I take my time with my most favourite painting at this gallery. The spinning girl in the dress.

"I see you have picked a favourite."

"I love this one, something about it communicates this feeling of…freedom. Like she has no inhibitions or diffidence."

I am looking at the painting and Seb is looking at me.

He doesn't meet my eyes and finds something thoroughly fascinating on the linoleum floor as he refuses to look back up at me.

"You want to say something but you're holding back," even after all these years I'm finely attuned to his tells.

"What if I tell you, that's you," he says, finally looking back at the painting, still not meeting my gaze.

I don't know what to make of his confession, how is this girl in a random painting…me?

"What do you mean, I'm confused."

"Teddy, this is mine. I painted this," he sighs and looks away again. "And you were my muse."

I am gobsmacked. I stutter a little but my vocal chords are unable to form any words. He painted a picture of me? Why? Why did I even cross his mind when we weren't in touch? I'm overwhelmed as I reach the same question I always land on when it comes to Seb, why didn't he tell me anything?

"S-sorry, I need to get out of here, I need to go," I excuse myself as I run out.

"Teddy, wait, please!" I can hear him come after me but I don't look back, I need to get out of this building.

I rush out of the glass doors into the compound. It's thundering and the rain could start any minute now. The area at the front is decorated with a blanket of twinkling, white fairy lights above, suspended in the air. They look blurry and hazy in my vision as water fills my eyes. The rain hasn't started yet, it's my tears obscuring my sight.

"Teddy, look at me," Seb catches up and turns me around as I continue sobbing.

No, I can't cry, I need to know everything. I need to know now.

"I'm sorry, Teddy"

"No! Tell me! Tell me why you left me like that!" I yell at him. "Tell me why you didn't bother telling me ANYTHING, Seb!"

"I'm sorry," he murmurs.

"No! Stop apologising for God's sake, fight with me Seb!" I scream and shake him by the shoulders. "Did our friendship mean nothing to you? Am I that dispensable, Seb? I am a good time until I'm not, right? I get it, I'm there for the galleries and museums and your fucking adventures, but when real life comes it's someone else." I shoot daggers and taste the venom in my voice.

"There's no one else, Teddy," he defends solemnly as his breathing increases rapidly.

"Then WHY? Tell me Seb, use your words, I'm going crazy here, do you even care?"

"Oh my God, because I love you goddammit!" He shouts in my face. "Because I loved you and I was dying and I thought I will never get to see you again and I loved you too much to put you through that too."

I stand motionless as I'm rendered speechless.

"They diagnosed me with stage two pancreatic cancer in the last month of my last year in uni. I don't know if you know but it's one of the rarer ones with the lowest fucking survival rate. I was so sure I was going to die Teddy," he laughs mirthlessly. "I loved you and I had wanted to tell you for months. Years, even. I knew you were special the first day I met you Teddy, it just took my brain some time to catch up to my heart. And by the time I was ready to say, fucking pancreas gave up on me. I didn't want our last memories to be tarnished by something so grim and terrible, something so opposite to what we shared. You were the most important person in my life, before I could die it was already killing me knowing I'll never get to see you again. I just didn't want to put you through that, you must understand."

"Why didn't you reach out after you got better?" I ask as I try to process everything he has just said.

"You weren't beholden to me Teddy, my life had been frozen as I got my treatment, I couldn't expect you to revert to a past version of yourself just to meet me where I was. You deserved to move on."

"I was going to tell you that I loved you that day, at your graduation."

"What?" He whispers.

"After your ceremony, I was going to tell you."

"Shit!" He ruffles his hair, now sopping wet with the rain that's pouring down on us.

"Why didn't you tell me sooner Seb, after we met again?"

"I tried Teddy! I was trying! But you were so elusive, you were avoiding me like the plague! It felt like everybody was getting the real Teddy and I was getting a shell of who you were!" He yells frustratedly.

"Well, I'm sorry, for having had bad experiences with people abandoning me like I am not valued at all!" I yell back.

"Sorry, I- I know where you're coming from."

"Sorry for yelling at you."

"I brought that out of you so I'll take the blame for that," he smiles.

The rain is still coming down on us at its full might. I don't move a muscle, except for my heart which is beating at a million kilometres per hour.

"You loved me?" I ask him.

"I love you. Present tense. If you let me."

"I love you too. Present tense. But I still need some time to like you again. It'll take some time before my fight and flight stops getting activated every time I see your face."

"That's alright, take all the time you need Teddy. I'm not leaving you this time."

He moves closer to me and asks and wordlessly asks for my permission as I nod. I meet him in the middle as he delicately places his hands on my cheeks and kisses me. I kiss him back, my hands automatically weaving into his hair in the back. We don't let go for what feels like eternity but I detach myself from him, running out of breath. We look at each other and can't help but laugh. He pulls me to him and kisses me again.

"You're stuck with me now," he says, punctuating each word with another kiss.

"Maybe I'll give you abandonment issues this time around," I fib jokingly.

"Don't you dare, Teddy," he says, tucking the wet strands of hair stuck to my cheeks behind my ear.

After all these years, once again, amidst London's rains, under twinkling lights he holds out his hand for me to hold. Intertwining our fingers, he lifts our hands and twirls me around. And maybe, just maybe, I believe in destiny and fate and the distinctly human act to believe in the universe's signs.

16

My smile is like I won a contest and to hide that would be so dishonest

1 year later

"Sissy, I can take Mia now," Millie asks for her daughter back from me, once again, as we are walking along the coast in Brighton. Seb and I are here to visit my sister and her family for the weekend.

"Why won't you let me and my niece be?" I ask her with a pout. "Why is your mommy being so possessive all of a sudden?" I ask Mia as she gives me a gummy laugh in return.

"Theadora Rossi."

"Woah, here take her, you don't have to use my government name," I say as I pass Mia back to her. "Where did that even come from?"

She huffs, "I just need you to be hands-free right now."

"Huh, why?"

She doesn't reply and keeps walking ahead. Why is she acting so strange? She has not shown any signs yet but I fear she may be an inch closer to becoming our mom after becoming a mom herself..

"Hurry up, Eric and Seb must be waiting for us."

Those two had taken off before us, something about going to a shop? I honestly don't know and I couldn't care, I practically tune out the rest of the world when I'm with my niece.

We reach an empty spot on the beach when Millie stops dead in her tracks. I don't know what's gotten into her as she gives me a creepy smile and yells "I love you, good luck" as she flees in the direction we just came from. What is going on? I turn back around and notice Seb coming towards me from behind a beach hut.

"Seb, what is happening, why is my sister behaving like a mad woman and why were you behind that hut and-"

My mouth stays wide open as Seb gets down on one knee and holds out a ring in a box.

"Teddy, I-"

"Yes! Yes, yes, yes, YES, YES!!!" I screech as I'm jumping up and down. "Yes, a hundred times over!" I cry out.

"Gosh, woman, let me ask the question first!"

"What's the point? I know the question, you know the answer, just put the ring on my finger!!!"

"No, please, I want to do this right Teddy."

"Ugh, fine, as you were."

"Teddy, I-"

"I heard her screaming yes!" Millie comes running back and tackles me in a hug. "I'm so happy for you two, congratulations! See, I told you you two were meant to be. It was written in the stars, you guys are soulmates, wait, why is the ring still in the box?"

"He hasn't technically proposed yet," I inform her.

"Those were some premature yesses that you heard," Seb added, still on his right knee on the stony Brighton beach. "I'm getting up now," he stands upright and before I can interrupt him anymore, he holds my face and blurts out, "Teddy, I want to spend every second of the rest of my life with you. You are my best friend and I truly believe my most beautiful memories with you are those of the future. I have loved you ever since I have known you, will you marry me and do me the honour of making me your husband?"

And no prizes for guessing what my answer was.

The end.

ACKNOWLEDGEMENTS

First and foremost, I want to express my deepest gratitude to my incredible parents. Their endless encouragement, unconditional love, and undying faith in me have been the driving force behind the creation of this book. Without their nudging, pushing, and, at times, shoving, I wouldn't have been able to bring these words to life.

To my best friends, Maha, Natalia, and Rati, your wildly eventful lives, the banter in our chats and more than a decade's worth of memories have been the wellspring of inspiration for the interactions between my characters. Thank you for always feeding into my delusions and unfounded confidence.

A heartfelt thank you goes out to my beta readers. Your dedication and invaluable feedback on the first draft of this book have been the cornerstone in shaping "For Old Times' Sake" into what it is today. Your insights and reactions have truly made a difference. Thank you to mitxeran for designing the beautiful cover and bringing my vision to life.

To Taylor Swift, though it's unlikely that you'll come across these words, your artistry and values have inspired me to write something I can proudly call my own.

Lastly, I want to express my appreciation to the booktok and bookstagram communities for reigniting my love for reading.

Thank you all for being a part of this journey.

ABOUT THE AUTHOR

A penchant for imagining fake scenarios and captivated by beautiful words and stories, it was only natural for Jahnvvi to find her way to writing fiction.

An ardent reader from a young age, after her studies at King's College London and a brief stint working in digital media marketing, Jahnvvi rediscovered her love for books and a desire to create something of her own.

A passionate fangirl who is immersed in pop culture lore, you will find her chronically online when she's not reading or writing.

For Old Times' Sake is her first book.

www.ingramcontent.com/pod-product-compliance
Lightning Source LLC
Chambersburg PA
CBHW020725160726
47993CB00006B/2353